SAWGRASS SLAUGHTER

There was another shot from a handgun, and this time Slocum got a fix on its location. The rifle boomed once more, and Slocum realized it was definitely a buffalo gun.

Suddenly, there was a flurry of motion in the grass. A man on his knees raised a pistol and pointed it toward the ridge, but his back exploded in a spray of gore that was still fanning out across the grass when the sound of the buffalo gun thundered through the valley.

"On the ridge," Slocum shouted. "Just caught a glimpse of him. Let's go!"

DON'T MISS THESE
ALL-ACTION WESTERN SERIES FROM
THE BERKLEY PUBLISHING GROUP

THE GUNSMITH by J. R. Roberts
Clint Adams was a legend among lawmen, outlaws, and ladies. They called him . . . the Gunsmith.

LONGARM by Tabor Evans
The popular long-running series about U.S. Deputy Marshal Long—his life, his loves, his fight for justice.

LONE STAR by Wesley Ellis
The blazing adventures of Jessica Starbuck and the martial arts master, Ki. Over eight million copies in print.

SLOCUM by Jake Logan
Today's longest-running action western. John Slocum rides a deadly trail of hot blood and cold steel.

JAKE LOGAN

SLOCUM AND THE WYOMING FRAME-UP

BERKLEY BOOKS, NEW YORK

SLOCUM AND THE WYOMING FRAME-UP

A Berkley Book / published by arrangement with
the author

PRINTING HISTORY
Berkley edition / October 1992

ISBN: 0-425-13472-5

A BERKLEY BOOK ® TM 757,375
Berkley Books are published by The Berkley Publishing Group,
200 Madison Avenue, New York, New York 10016.
The name "BERKLEY" and the "B" logo
are trademarks belonging to Berkley Publishing Corporation.

PRINTED IN THE UNITED STATES OF AMERICA
10 9 8 7 6 5 4 3 2 1

SLOCUM AND THE WYOMING FRAME-UP

1

The sky looked like the deepest water Slocum had ever seen. It was so blue, he had the distinct sensation he could reach out with a finger and start a ripple that would go on forever. A Wyoming autumn was something that had to be seen to be believed. The clouds, few and widely spaced, looked like puffs of the purest, softest cotton. He could barely keep his eyes off the heavens as he rode along behind the chuck wagon.

The rest of the hands of the Double Deuce ranch seemed not to notice. Slocum didn't know whether he was being silly, or if after a while he, like the other hands, would begin to take the incredible sight for granted. He hoped he would always be able to respond to something as beautiful as that September sky.

The rest of the hands were out in front of the chuck wagon, more intent on getting to their work, as if it were more meaningful than the broad blue expanse above them. Maybe it was, Slocum thought. Maybe getting your hands dirty, working until your shoulders ached and your back refused to bend was what really mattered.

Feeling like he was being unsociable, he spurred his chestnut and moved on past the chuck wagon, waving to Cookie Mercer as he passed. The old man waved one nicotine-stained hand at him, shouted something Slocum didn't catch, and showed most of the teeth he had left in a fit of silent laughter.

Up ahead, Ben Donaldson was riding point. It seemed as if the foreman were running a race. As soon as a couple of the hands drew close, he would lash his big bay gelding with the reins, once on each side, and spurt ahead a few yards. Donaldson never looked back, and didn't wave as if to challenge the other hands to keep up, but they all seemed to sense that that was what he had in mind.

The creaking of the wagon springs began to fall away behind Slocum as he raced to catch up. He glanced back once, drawing a wave from Mercer, then fixed his eyes on the broad back of Dave Duncan, the last man in line behind Donaldson, except for himself.

It was going to be a long four weeks, but Slocum felt like he needed something as intense and as protracted as this work detail promised to be. He had been drifting for so long, hardly ever staying in any one place long enough to learn the names of the endless number of towns in which he had spent a night—or two or three— as often as not, working for just three square meals and a roof for the night. And more often than he cared to remember, the roof leaked and the food went down hard.

The Double Deuce seemed like it might be the answer to a range rider's prayer, a place where he could do honest work for honest pay for just about as long as he cared to break a sweat. Or as long as he was able. He didn't mind work. Hell, it was about the only thing in his life that had never let him down. He had a past he didn't like to think about, and a future barely certain enough to warrant consideration, so the day-to-day was where he kept his focus. It was like an anchor for him.

Every sunrise was followed by a sunset, and that was about as predictable as his life had ever been. He didn't want it to be that way necessarily, but it just seemed to happen. It was like someone had mapped it all out without consulting him, then left it for him to figure out if he could. So far he hadn't figured out much.

Georgia, wherein lay his few and progressively more feeble roots, was nearly two thousand miles and a half-dozen years behind him now. There was nothing left for him there: no family, no friends, nothing to go back to. But he couldn't go back, even if he had a reason, because there was a price on his head. Or at least there had been when he left. Most likely he was little more than a fading memory to the people in the red clay country now, if they remembered him at all.

He was almost even with Dave Duncan now, and the big, friendly hand flashed him a grin as he started to draw a little bit ahead. "What's your hurry, John?" Duncan hollered. "The work ain't going nowhere."

"It won't get done until we get to it either, Dave," Slocum shouted back.

"God, how the boss must love you, Slocum. You're one eager sumbitch."

"I got empty pockets, Davey."

"Hell, we all do, John. That don't mean you have to work like a slave." But he laughed. The boss was Dan McCrae, the owner of the Double Deuce, and he was widely regarded as one of the easiest-going men within a hundred miles of Cheyenne. He was also one of the wealthiest, and conventional wisdom had it that the size of McCrae's bank account made it just a mite easier to be happy-go-lucky. Whatever the reason, he had an easy rapport with his men, never pushed them too hard, and treated them fairly as long as they returned the favor. He could be hard-nosed, especially in business, but Slocum hadn't heard a single nasty comment about McCrae in the three weeks he'd been on board the Double Deuce. That alone was enough to stamp McCrae as remarkable.

They still had three miles to go before they reached Bracken's Creek, where the month's labor was to start.

Already there—at least everyone hoped—were several wagons loaded with fence posts and barbed wire. McCrae, like most of his neighbors, was concerned about the damage sheep were doing to the grazing land. He wanted to fence in as much as he could before the cold weather came. Once the winter freeze set in, the ground would be rock solid and putting posts in would be impossible until spring.

During September they would put in posts and run wire at the same time. It wouldn't be fun, but after September they would plant fence posts as long as the weather permitted, then run wire until the first snow. The men could run wire even in subfreezing temperatures, but the snow would pile up in shoulder-high drifts—maybe even higher—and the posts would be hidden until the spring thaw.

Slocum patted his hip pocket, suddenly afraid that he might have left his gloves behind. Digging the post holes would tear his hands up badly enough even with the gloves, and the wire barbs would shred the raw flesh to mincemeat without them. The gloves were there, and he relaxed a little, still urging his mount to gain on the rest of the work crew.

Duncan yelled something he didn't catch, and Slocum turned to see the big kid laughing at him. Slocum was feeling pretty lucky. It had been a while since he'd had steady work, and the Double Deuce was a nice place. Unlike most crews, Donaldson and the rest of the hands on McCrae's spread were open, even friendly. They still ragged the newcomer as if he were a rookie, but it lacked the hard edge most crews seemed to have. It had always struck Slocum that ranch hands had two ways of dealing with a stranger—they either rode him unmercifully, as if they thought he was after their jobs, or they ignored him totally, as if to pretend he wasn't there, which was as good as his not being there in reality.

Slocum had learned to live with that sort of treatment, but he didn't like it, and made a point to go out of his way for anyone who joined a crew after he did.

Work was hard enough without being made to feel like a leper.

He could see the canvas tops of the supply wagons now, four of them, which meant there were four wagons full of wire rolls. The other wagons, full of rough-hewn fence posts, were still below the horizon, but as he pushed on he could see one, higher up the slope than the others, begin to materialize out of the shimmering haze. The air looked like water, and just above the ground it was so hot already that it blurred everything seen through it.

Donaldson spurred his horse now, and the big chestnut leaped ahead as the foreman broke over the ridgeline and started down toward the creek. As Slocum followed him over the hilltop, he saw the meandering band of cottonwoods along the streambed. Glints of sunlight off the water, filtered somewhat by the leaves, flashed back at him, and he was suddenly thirsty.

He could see all the wagons now—ten of them, counting the four full of wire—and the magnitude of the job ahead hit home. Just thinking about it made his back hurt and shoulders sag. The Double Deuce was one of the largest spreads in the territory, and the thought of fencing it in was staggering. McCrae was going to start slowly, trying out a new kind of wire that some traveling drummer had sold him at a discount. If it worked, there'd be a lot more to buy, miles of it to string three strands high along the entire perimeter of the Double Deuce.

It would cost a fortune, but there seemed to be no way around the expense. The sheep, which were multiplying almost weekly, cropped the buffalo grass right down to the roots, often damaging the plants so badly that a prolonged dry spell would kill them altogether. And even when the plants survived, the sheep left a stink the cattle hated. They wouldn't graze on sheep land no matter how hungry they were.

Like most of the cattlemen in the area, Dan McCrae was boiling mad about the influx of sheep men, but the government was trying to encourage settlement, giving

the sheepherders a lot of incentives. Slocum had seen
range wars before, and he hoped to God he wasn't about
to see another one. It was usually the most vulnerable on
both sides who got hurt, leaving the most brutal cattlemen squared off against the most stubborn of the sheep
men. All the reasonable folks in the middle seemed to
vanish like smoke on a stiff breeze.

And that's when it got really bad. That was when
homes were burned, stock slaughtered, and men started
sniping at one another.

Slocum hoped it wouldn't come to that in Bracken
County. From what he'd seen of the Double Deuce
hands, it would take a lot to push them to that sort
of frenzy. But there were no guarantees, and he knew
that, too.

The first gunshot came out of the blue. It echoed, seeming to bounce off the sky, and Slocum saw Donaldson's
head snap around, trying to pinpoint the location. Three
more shots, close together, exploded, each drowning out
the echo of the one before it. Then two more were heard.
Donaldson spurred his mount into a gallop then, and
changed direction. He angled toward a break in the trees,
barely slowing as he crossed Bracken's Creek, and started
up the opposite slope. Slocum kicked his chestnut and
lashed it with the reins. The other hands thundered along
in his wake. The shots had come from somewhere on the
far side of the ridge, probably halfway up the hill.

Donaldson was nearly at the top now, and Slocum
was right on his tail. They broke over the crest of the
hill almost simultaneously. The gunman was already
climbing up the far hill, and Donaldson shouted, then
drew his gun and fired two warning shots, but the rider
never looked back. He disappeared over the next ridge,
leaving a swirl of dust behind him.

Donaldson reined in, not knowing whether to chase
the rider, having seen no sign so far of what his target might have been. There was no law against target
practice or just plain old Fourth of July gunfire, even in
September. Maybe the man was drunk. Maybe he was

crazy. No law against either, Slocum thought. He reined in beside Donaldson.

"What the hell was that all about, I wonder," Slocum said.

"Beats me, John. I reckon somebody's mad at his wife and blew off a little steam. Sure wasn't shootin' at us, far as I can tell."

"Seems like he wasn't shooting at anything," Slocum said.

Dave Duncan moved in alongside Slocum. "Guess again," he said, pointing toward a clump of brush on the floor of the vee-shaped valley. "What the hell you think that is down there in them shadows? It's something, that much I know."

Donaldson shook his head. "Got no idea, Davey. Why don't you and Slocum here go check it out. The rest of you boys git on back to them wagons. We got work to do."

Slocum nudged his horse into a walk and started toward the brush, and Duncan fell in beside him, staying on the uphill side of the chestnut.

As they got closer, there was still nothing much to see, just some scrub oak and young willows, probably rooted around a small spring or a sinkhole. Dark shadows massed at the base of the willows, but there was nothing much else to see. Fifty yards from the willows, Slocum swung out of the saddle and handed the reins of the chestnut to Duncan. "Hang on a minute. I'll go take a closer look," he said.

The grass was knee-high, dry as old bones, and hissed against his jeans as he strode downhill the last thirty yards. A fine powdery dust rose off the dry blades and insects swarmed in angry clouds, swirling like small tornadoes for a few seconds, then settling down as Slocum moved past.

He could smell something now, something almost sweet and definitely out of place.

He sensed something and stopped, his right hand settling on the butt of his Colt Navy.

"What's wrong?" Duncan hollered.

Slocum shook his head uncertainly. "Not sure," he shouted back. He started forward again, this time easing the Colt from its holster. Stepping into the brush, he swept a branch to one side with his left arm, then froze again.

"What'd you find?" Duncan shouted, urging his mount down the hill, tugging Slocum's along in his wake.

"Cows," Slocum said. "Six of 'em. All dead."

"Bad water?" Duncan asked, slipping from the saddle.

"Worse than that," Slocum said. "They got bullet holes in their skulls."

2

Ben Donaldson came roaring down the slope on foot, Dave Duncan right behind him. "Sonofabitch," Donaldson was shouting, over and over, until the individual words were lost in the Gatling gun repetition. They were reduced to a stream of rage. He tripped in the tall grass, sprawled forward several yards, and it seemed to Slocum that he clawed his way forward several body lengths while scrambling back to his feet.

By the time he reached the clump of brush, his face was beet-red under his tan, and his breath was coming in short, spasmodic gasps. "Where are they, John?" he asked, swallowing hard and patting his chest as if to calm his heart.

Slocum led him into the brush without a word, pointed to the six carcasses, and stepped aside as Donaldson placed one huge hand on his shoulder to make room for himself.

The foreman squatted beside the nearest dead steer, and for a long time he said nothing. In the silence, the buzz of flies seemed to grow louder. Several were already clustered around the bullet hole in the steer's skull, glistening brilliant blue and green. They looked almost like some sort of brooch, as if the animal had been decorated with an old woman's most prized heirloom. Then Donaldson reached out with a gloved hand, brushed the flies away and said, "Looks like .44 caliber."

He turned then to look back over his shoulder at Slocum and Duncan. "Why in hell would anybody do such a thing?"

Slocum shrugged. Duncan shifted his feet, but had no answer. Instead, he said, "I reckon it was them gunshots we heard when we got to the wagons. The blood's still fresh."

"Course it was, Davey. I know *when* it happened. What I don't know is why? Nothing like this ever happened before. Not around here, anyhow."

"Them sheepherders, maybe."

Donaldson waved a hand in disgust. "Naw, they know better'n that. The last thing they want is a range war. There has to be some other reason."

"Well, I'm fresh out," Duncan said. "If it wasn't them, then I don't have any idea who coulda done it."

"I wish to God we had chased that bastard," Donaldson said. "But it's too late now. Whoever he is, he's long gone." The foreman straightened up then and moved around the carcass. He glanced quickly at the other five bodies, his head nodding as if in time to some inaudible music. He checked the brands and the earmarks on all six, then said, "Mr. McCrae ain't gonnna like this one single bit."

"He don't have to know, Ben," Duncan said.

Donaldson looked up sharply. "The hell he don't. I got a responsibility to that man. I can't hide nothing from him. Especially not something like this."

"Aw, hell, Ben. We lose steers all the time. He don't know how many he's got. What's a half-dozen one way or the other?"

"There's a difference, Davey. And I do know how many he's got," Donaldson said.

"Oh yeah, how many?"

"Six less than he had last night. That's how many. And I'm telling you right now, Davey. You ever hide something like this from me and I find out about it, you'll be one sorry pup. You understand what I'm telling you?"

Duncan looked at the ground for a moment, scratched at the dry ground with one toe, then shook his head. "Yes, sir," he mumbled.

"I can't hear you, Davey."

"I said yes, sir, Ben."

"I mean it, now."

Duncan nodded again. "I know you do. I know it, Ben. Don't worry about me."

Donaldson nodded. "Make sure I don't have to." He turned to Slocum then. "How good are you at tracking, Slocum?"

"I'm not an Apache, but I'm not bad."

"Why I ask, the rest of these boys can't find their ass with both hands. I got to stay here and make sure they don't nail themselves to the fence posts, so I can't do it myself."

"You want me to see if I can pick up the trail the gunman left?"

Donaldson nodded again. "That I do. But you listen here," he said, wagging a finger under Slocum's nose. "Don't you do nothing stupid. You find him if you can, see where he went, where he lives if he's from around here, but don't you do nothing else. Don't you try to bring him in by yourself. Understood?"

"Don't worry, Mr. Donaldson, I'll be careful."

"It's Ben, damn it. You're pretty near as old as I am. No need for you to be callin' me Mister. Besides, none of these other boys do. No point in stickin' out like a sore thumb, is there?"

"Whatever you say, Ben."

"Get going, and see what you can find out. I'll be here the next few days, so come on back here instead of the bunkhouse when you're done. And if you lose 'im, don't worry about it. The ground's pretty dry and there ain't much chance you'll be able to find him."

Slocum rubbed a gloved hand across his brow, looked for a moment at the smear of sweat on the leather, then moved toward his horse. He swung into the saddle, flipped a salute at Donaldson, and walked the chestnut toward the spot where he remembered seeing the gunman charge up the slope.

He heard a nicker as Donaldson and Duncan reached the top of the hill and mounted their horses. He glanced back, saw Duncan wave, and then fixed his eyes on the ground. There wasn't much of a chance, he knew. The ground was dry and had been for quite a while. Even a fresh hoofprint was unlikely to turn up in dry earth, so each print would likely resemble every other. But he was glad to get away from the prospect of raw palms and aching shoulders, so he'd give it a try.

The grass was bent in some places and he slipped from the saddle to examine the crushed blades. Some of them oozed a yellowish-green fluid, which meant they had to have been recently broken. That would be all right for a couple of hours, but as soon as the sun was high in the sky, the grass would dry and he'd be back to looking at the dusty earth for traces of the gunman.

Looking up the slope, he could see the line of bent grass, and climbed back into the saddle. He wanted to make as much time as he could before the sun turned against him. At the top of the slope he looked back down and saw the two lines of broken grass, the one made by his own mount and that left by the gunman. The rider's trail slashed on an angle across the slope, straight as an arrow out of the clump of brush.

On the hilltop he dismounted again, walking along with the chestnut trailing behind him. He spotted the continuation of the line all the way down to a narrow creek on the valley floor. Remounting, Slocum rode slowly down the side of the hill, conscious that there was good cover on the far side, and that anyone hidden there wouldn't be visible until he was almost on top of him. He doubted the gunman would have holed up this close, but he wasn't anxious to stop a bullet, and yanked his carbine from its boot, levered a shell home, and kept the Winchester balanced across his saddle horn.

The sun was climbing higher, and the morning haze was starting to burn off. There was a harsh glare that caused him to squint as he scanned the creek bank. Sweat was starting to trickle down his back, and he could feel his shirt getting clammy and sticking to his skin in patches across his shoulders and back.

A sudden movement off to the right caught his eye, and he swung the Winchester toward the brush. Tempted to dismount and approach on foot, he slowed the chestnut to a walk. When there was no further movement, he stayed in the saddle, keeping a tight rein on the horse and his eyes pinned on the now motionless brush.

The chestnut nickered, as if it scented something, and Slocum reined in. A moment later, something he couldn't quite make out dashed through the brush. It wasn't a man, he was sure of that. The brush grew still again, until the horse nickered once more, shuffling its feet and trying to move sidewise, as if ready to bolt.

Once more the brush rustled, and again he saw whatever it was, just patches of gray visible through the leaves. Slocum gave a shrill whistle, and the gray thing exploded out of the brush on the far side of the creek. He swung the Winchester up even before his eyes fixed on the animal. It was a wolf, and it was limping badly.

Slocum took aim, squeezed the trigger gently, and the Winchester bucked against his shoulder. The sharp smell of gunsmoke swirled around him. He saw the wolf's hindquarters jolt to the left, then collapse. The animal pawed at the ground for a few moments, dragging itself toward the tall grass, but its strength deserted it. It moaned softly once, then lay still.

Slocum nudged the chestnut with his knees and the horse trotted the rest of the way downhill, hesitated for a moment at the creek bank, then stepped down into the shallow water and waded across. Slocum rode the seventy yards or so to where the wolf lay in short grass and dismounted.

He saw a trail of blood on the ground, too long to have been from the bullet wound. The wolf had been hurt before. Nudging the carcass with one toe, he rolled it over and saw a jagged wound in the animal's belly. It looked as if something had torn it open. Squatting to take a closer look, he examined the wolf closely, thinking it may have had a run-in with another of its own kind or with a bear. But the wound didn't fit either explanation. It was more like a single thing had ripped at the underbelly of the wolf, not jaws or the razor claws of a grizzly.

Straightening up, Slocum followed the trail of fresh blood back into the brush. He moved cautiously, not wanting to stumble unexpectedly on whatever it was that had done in the wolf. He thumbed back the carbine's hammer, then pushed aside some scrub oak branches with his left arm.

There was more blood on the grass beside the creek, and he followed it several yards, stepping into the water and walking downstream to make sure he had room to swing the carbine muzzle quickly. His feet splashed in the six-inch deep water. He bent down, snatched a rock from under the water and tossed it into the brush.

The brush exploded as several crows fluttered through the brush and out into the hot sun, squawking and beating their enormous wings. He knew wolves usually traveled in packs, but didn't hear anything to suggest more of the animals were hidden in the undergrowth.

He took another three steps, and then saw what had drawn the wolf—and the crows. Three more steers lay in a heap on the creek bank, their heads bobbing in the water and still trailing pink swirls in the sluggish current.

The biggest lay on its side, one horn smeared with blood. That explained the nearly gutted wolf. It must have stumbled on the wounded animals and gotten too close too soon. A flick of the steer's head must have caught the wolf unexpectedly, maybe tossed it into the brush.

Slocum bent over to look more closely. As with the six animals from earlier that day, each showed a single bullet wound in the head. He hadn't heard the shots, so it must have happened not long after the first incident, maybe even before.

He looked around in the grass, saw a couple of partial bootprints, and leaned over them. In the shade along the creek he couldn't see them clearly, but there really wasn't much to see. There was nothing odd about the partial prints; no unusual cut mark in either the sole or the heel, nothing he could use to identify the boot.

Something glittered in the water. He thought for a moment a fish had broken the surface, but when he moved his head, he could see that the glitter was motionless, something lying in the water. Moving closer, he leaned over and scooped it up. A shell casing, .44 caliber Remington. But it, too, was almost useless. There must be 10,000 guns in Wyoming Territory that could have fired the shell.

Tucking the casing in his shirt pocket, he moved on past the carcasses and, when nothing else caught his eye, he eased through the brush and into the grass. A single line through the grass on the hillside was still his only real lead.

It was going to be a long day.

3

Slocum followed the trail for another eight miles. The ground was starting to get rocky, and the hoofprints fainter and fainter. The dry earth was tough enough, but with slabs of rock and loose scree covering large patches of ground, it was even tougher. Here and there he found a freshly broken stone, some of which could have been shattered by a horseshoe, but he was growing less and less certain whether he was following a trail.

Scanning the rough terrain ahead from one edge of the horizon to the other, he saw nothing that even hinted of the presence of another man. It was tempting to pack it in and head back. Even the thought of struggling with posts and barbed wire under the harsh glare of the sun wasn't much of a deterrent.

A mile or so ahead, the ground sloped downward, and off to the left he saw a gap in the rocks that might be a small opening into a box canyon. Water rushed through the opening and turned white as it tumbled over stones and wound across the rocky floor. That was as far as he was prepared to go, and he nudged the chestnut into a trot. Keeping as much as possible to the patches of grass, he skirted the exposed slabs of rock and made his way down the slope.

On the way down, he didn't turn up a single sign of recent passage, but he was so close he figured he might as well check the gap in the rock face, just to be sure.

As he closed on the opening, the click of his mount's horseshoes echoing back at him from the stony face on either side, he slowed, then dismounted with less than fifty yards to go. There was still no sign of anyone as he tied the chestnut to a small cottonwood sapling that had managed somehow to take root in the stony floor of the broad valley.

Once more, he pulled out the Winchester, and headed toward the opening in the rock. The stream was nearly thirty feet across, and rather deep. Its excited burble as it gushed over and around the larger stones in its bed grew louder as he neared the gap in the rock wall.

The opening was wider than it had seemed. He realized as he neared it that because of the angle of his approach he had been looking at it from the side. A narrow strip of ground led inside, but to get to it he'd have to wade across the fast-moving water. Stepping down into it, he felt the cold water seep into his boots. His legs grew heavy with the chill as he hauled first one foot and then the other out of the stream to make his way across. Toward the middle it was nearly waist-deep. The cool water felt almost pleasant after a bit, except for his feet, which were starting to numb.

Reaching the strip of rocky ground on the other side of the stream, he ducked into a crouch and dashed to the wall, flattening himself against it to listen. He half expected to hear the crack of a rifle from somewhere inside, but nothing happened. All he could hear was the rushing water and, almost drowned by the noisy stream, the sound of his own breathing.

After a minute, he edged close to the opening and peered around the sheer face of the rock. As he'd guessed, it was a small box canyon, no more than three hundred feet deep and less than half that wide. At the back end, water cascaded over the lip of the canyon, then fell two-thirds of the way down onto a huge boulder tucked in one corner. The water then bubbled up and over the rock, spreading itself in a broad sheet as it fell to the canyon floor.

He could see the stream funnel toward a narrow channel, where it deepened and charged straight across the canyon toward the exit. Most of the canyon floor was dry, littered with flakes of rock and brittle-edged slabs of reddish stone, in some places stacked haphazardly, looking much like a pile of books knocked over by a careless librarian.

Slocum ducked as low as he could and darted through the opening. Inside, he dove behind one of the stone slabs and lay still, once more listening for some indication that he'd been noticed. After three minutes, he decided the canyon must be deserted and got to his knees. Leaning on the stone slab, he surveyed the canyon, one wall at a time, looking for anything at all to tell him whether someone was—or recently had been— there.

He started noting details now, clumps of brush hard against the walls, where they could escape the crush of rocks tumbling into the canyon. There was even a large patch of green toward the right, where it could get sunlight much of the day. The walls themselves were almost straight, a hundred feet high, maybe a little more. No path marked any of them, meaning the opening behind him was the only way in or out without a rope.

Cautiously, Slocum stood up. "Hello!" he shouted. His own voice boomed back at him from a dozen directions. It sounded even louder than the initial yell as its echoes swarmed around him like hornets. There was no answer, but he hadn't really expected one.

Once more, he called, "Anyone here?"

Again, the call fractured into a cloud of echoes and swirled around him, one last, dying echo heard once, then again, and then gone.

He thumbed the hammer back on the Winchester and moved out from behind the rock. He had called and no one answered, so anyone in here was either deaf or fair game. Since his life would depend on it, he chose the latter assumption as he threaded his way among the stones.

The ground was clear along the deep channel, which barely contained the rushing water, and he followed it, still crouched. His eyes swept from side to side, turning to check behind him every few steps. He felt just the least bit silly, and wondered what someone on the rimrock would have thought of his wary ballet. He smiled, laughed softly at himself, then shrugged off the sense of foolishness.

When he reached the huge boulder, shrouded in cascading water, he stopped to look all around the rim, paying particular attention to the wall just above the opening into the canyon. Anyone arriving after him could have seen his horse and ridden up to the rim. But it was just as vacant as the other three walls. He was alone.

He was about to turn and go, when he smelled something. He couldn't identify it at first, but knew it was out of place. The air around him was full of fine mist from the waterfall, but he knew he had scented something that didn't belong, that wasn't part of the canyon's normal aroma.

Taking a deep breath, he could almost taste it; bitter—dark and bitter. Then he knew what it was: ash, charcoal. Somewhere there had been a fire, and not that long ago. With renewed interest he moved along the back wall of the canyon, stepping over a cluster of small boulders, then around the side of a tall slab standing almost on end and leaning against another. And that's where he found it. The remains of small campfire. There was a lot of ash, despite the small size of the blaze, which told him the site had been used repeatedly, probably by one or, at the most, two men.

Small stones had been arranged in a rough circle to contain the blaze, and the area around it was littered with cigarette butts. A quick survey of the surrounding area showed no sign of supplies, and gave no suggestion that the camper or campers would be returning anytime soon.

On the off chance, he knelt, spread his hand over the ashes and lowered it gently. There was no heat. The ashes were stone cold. Shaking his head, he got to his feet again. Now he had two questions—who had made the camp, and was there a connection to the dead stock or was this just a coincidence?

It crossed his mind that he might wait a day, or even two, camp someplace outside the box canyon and keep a close watch on it. He had tried to be cautious in his tracking, but there was no guarantee that the man he'd been following hadn't spotted him. It was always the chance you took, and as often as not, you lost. But if he had been spotted, his quarry had shown no inclination to bushwhack him. So he could count himself lucky on that score, anyhow.

As quickly as the idea had come to him, he dismissed it. Dan McCrae wasn't paying him to be a stock detective. He was getting paid to work the Double Deuce, and at the moment that meant fencing grazing land with the rest of the hands. If the campsite was connected, the sheriff could look into it, or McCrae could hire a regulator to ride herd on the stock butcher, whoever he was.

Slocum lowered the Winchester, eased the hammer down with his thumb, and looked up at the rimrock one last time. The edge of the canyon was as deserted as it had been ten minutes before. Sharp as a razor, the broken rock sliced across the brilliant blue far above, and stone and sky looked so close the canyon walls might have been holding up the heavens. The sun was almost dead overhead, an unblinking eye staring down at him with a concentration that was almost malevolent.

He started back toward the mouth of the canyon. He still swiveled his head back and forth, but he was now convinced that the canyon was deserted. The Winchester swung from his right fist, its muzzle pointed at the ground. Realizing he was thirsty, he stopped, dropped to his knees, and leaned over the swift current of the creek.

Setting the carbine to one side, placing it carefully so it wouldn't slide off the rock and into the water, he tugged off his gloves, cupped his hands and dipped them into the water. His hands were cold almost instantly, and when he sucked the water into his mouth, it made his teeth ache. He spat the first mouthful back into the current, watched the little swirl of dust and bubbles vanish under the surface, and took a second mouthful. He swallowed this one, then refilled his hands.

On the surface of the current, he could see the sun in the sky behind him, but it didn't hurt his eyes, because it reflected up and away from him. He was even thirstier than he had realized, he thought, as he gulped the water down, ignoring the numbness of his cheeks and the biting pain in his jawbone.

When he had drunk his fill, he reached for the gloves, tucked them into his jeans pocket, then closed his fingers around the Winchester.

The first crack took him by surprise. He jerked his head around, looking for the gunman, but saw no one. He started to get to his feet when the rifle cracked again, this time off to his left. He flattened himself and rolled, but the nearest cover was several yards behind him.

And the third shot slammed into him, hitting him on the fleshy part of his left arm, and he tumbled forward into the creek, partly from the impact and partly by design. There was nowhere else to hide.

Ducking to keep his head just below the edge of the streambed, he groped for the Winchester, found the barrel, and flinched when the fourth shot exploded. Something bit into his hands, probably a sliver of rock, and he jerked his hand toward him and down into the water.

Whoever was gunning for him wasn't the greatest shot in the world, but he had all day, and Slocum was going nowhere without exposing himself to the sniper.

His legs stretched out behind him in the water, and they were already beginning to go numb. He had to get out, but how? His arm throbbed, and he took a peek. The wound was through and through, and the water around him was dark red, as if someone had emptied a cask of wine somewhere upstream.

He'd have to leave the Winchester, which put him at a real disadvantage. Without a long gun, he had no way to keep the sniper honest. But there was nothing else he could do. Waiting for dark was out of the question. Rolling toward the center of the creek, he pointed his head toward the opening of the canyon, stretched his arms out and let the current start to move him. He used his legs and feet to keep himself steady in the water, turning his head to one side to gulp fresh air, then burying his face in the current and pushing himself along a few body lengths.

He heard a bullet slam into the water dangerously close to him, but kept on pushing. It was his only chance.

Gasping for air once more, it looked as if he were no closer to the canyon's mouth, but he knew he had to have covered some ground. It was taking forever. Plunging ahead, he moved more toward the center of the creek, and away from the rocky bank which gave him some cover, but he had to get into deeper water. Using his one good arm now, he hauled himself along and suddenly felt the bottom of the creek fall away from his fingertips.

Slocum started to swim as one more bullet sailed past him, plunking into the water just inches away from his head. The current was stronger here, and he tried to ignore the numbness in his wounded arm and the leaden feeling in his remaining limbs. Spluttering and gasping, he saw the entrance approaching and let the swiftness of the current carry him out and through it into shallow water.

His Colt Navy would probably be useless, the cartridges full of sodden gunpowder now. He staggered to his feet and started to sprint toward the chestnut, but the horse looked as if it were a mile away. He had more cartridges in his saddlebags, and another gun, a Colt Peacemaker.

As he stumbled ahead, he kept waiting for the shot he wouldn't hear, the bullet that would plow into him ahead of the sound of its discharge, but he reached the chestnut and fell to his knees beside it.

Snatching at the reins, he tugged them free from the brush and hauled himself into the saddle.

4

Slocum's arm felt as if someone were twisting a red-hot poker in the muscle. The piercing waves of pain kept him awake as he leaned over the pommel of his saddle, trying desperately to hold on. He felt the blood soaking his sleeve, and glancing at the arm he could no longer see the color of the shirt through the sticky mess. He had to stop the bleeding before he lost consciousness, but didn't know whether he was being followed or not.

A mile or so ahead, a stand of cottonwoods, just a few and most of them scraggly, shimmered in the heat. As he tried to open his eyes wider, forcing them to focus as best he could, he realized he wasn't sure how many trees there were. Was it six—or twelve? He tried waving a hand in front of his face, and found that he no longer remembered how many fingers he was supposed to have.

Waves of nausea swept over him, and he knew that he was close to losing consciousness. The hell with cover, he thought, jerking the reins and cooing softly for the chestnut to slow down. He felt himself falling to the left, and tried to wrap the reins in his fist to make certain the horse didn't run off too far for him to catch it.

He managed to break his fall with one leg, twisting it under him as he slipped from the saddle. He lay there for a long moment, his head swimming. The sun was hammering him, but chills wracked his body, and he started to shiver. He stared up at the sun wondering where its heat had gone. He heard a voice and his head wobbled unsteadily on his spine as he tried to sit up to see who had spoken to him. By the time he realized there was no one, that he had mumbled something aloud to himself, he was back flat on the ground. He could barely feel the sharp stones poking into his shoulder blades and hips, and one fist-sized rock lodged in the small of his back. He tried to shift his position to relieve the discomfort, then swallowed hard, his dry throat barely permitting the empty gesture.

He wanted to rip off the good sleeve of his shirt to tie it around the wounded arm, but he lacked the strength. He tried rending the cloth with his teeth, but couldn't get a grip on the faded cotton. His fingers fumbled then with the buttons and he rolled on his stomach when the last one came free. Taking a deep breath and closing his eys to ward off the dizziness caused by the exertion, he managed to get the dry sleeve off. Tossing the bulk of the shirt over to the other side of his body, he started to slide it down his wounded arm, steeling himself for the flash of pain he feared would come if the cloth was tangled in the raw wound.

But the shirt slid on down the arm without a hitch. He tried once more to sit up and this time managed it. He propped himself up with his good arm and peered like a drunk down over his shoulder at the bullet hole in the upper arm. The front was ragged, where the bullet had passed through, pushing flesh ahead of it. He tried to move the arm to get a peek at the entrance wound in back, but the movement seared him. He cried out and let the arm fall to his side again.

He had lost quite a lot of blood, that much he knew. As for the rest, he could only guess. As far as he could determine, the bullet had not struck bone. No major vein or artery seemed to have been severed, despite the mess, and he supposed he should count himself lucky to be alive. Three or four inches to the left, and he'd have been a dead man, lying there with one arm dangling in the freezing water of the creek.

But he was alive, for a while at least, and if he wanted to stay that way, he had to do two things: he had to stop the bleeding and get the hell out of there.

He took the shirt in his good hand and wrapped it around the wounded arm, trying three times before managing to loop the sleeve around itself. He stuffed one end into his mouth, bit down hard, and jerked the other end. He felt the sleeve tighten over the wound, and one more time the poker burned him to the bone. He groaned through the balled cotton in his mouth, looped the rest of the sleeve around for one more loop, pulled it tight, and lay back to regain his composure.

He could see the chestnut standing a couple of yards away, the reins dragging on the ground, keeping one eye on him as it nuzzled some bunch grass from a crevice in the rocky ground.

Taking several deep breaths, he sat up for the second time, rolled up on one hip and managed to get on his knees. He inched with painful slowness closer to the reins, reached for them and almost lost his balance. He caught himself with the hand of his good arm, but the shock sent another ball of fire shooting through his left arm. Panting like a thirsty mongrel, he moved still closer, managed to tangle the reins in his outstretched fingers, and held on for dear life. He tugged gently, and the chestnut eyed him curiously, tried to toss its head, felt the tug and shuffled closer to him.

When he could reach a stirrup, Slocum used it to haul himself erect, then leaned against the animal for a minute or so, his panting breath further drying his already parched throat. When he had the strength, he got a foot in the stirrup and half pulled and half threw himself up over the saddle, balancing on his stomach for several seconds before finding the strength to swing a leg up and over.

He was in the saddle, he thought, searching for the other stirrup with his right leg. Now, all he had to do was stay there. And move the horse, and stay awake long enough to find his way back to the work detail. That presumed whoever had shot at him wasn't already on his tail, waiting for a chance to finish the job.

He reached for the leather strap holding his canteen on the saddle horn, found it, yanked the canteen up and fumbled with the screw top. The top was held on by a small chain, its links dulled by years of use, whitened with metal salts. The cap clanked against the canvas covered side as he hoisted the canteen to his lips. He took a long drink, felt the parchment lining his throat dissolve, and took a deep breath.

Slocum screwed the cap back on, looped the strap over the pommel again, and let the canteen slap the chestnut's side. Pulling on the reins, fighting another wave of dizziness, this one not nearly so severe, he urged the chestnut to turn around and aimed for the cottonwoods. He tried to listen for the sounds of pursuit, but his ears were buzzing, and the blood left in his veins drummed and hammered, drowning out all other sound.

He squeezed the chestnut with his knees then, and got the animal into a walk. He wanted to go faster, afraid the sun would fry his brains as it scorched his back, but if the chestnut were moving too fast, he feared he might fall from the saddle.

He rode for hours, the plodding gait of the horse lulling him, the monotonous swaying in the saddle somehow not tossing him free. He curled his fingers in the chestnut's mane, tangling the reins in among the flesh and hair, making a knot of them all in hopes of keeping himself on board.

Once he almost lost his grip, started to slip, as if nodding off, and barely caught himself in time. The sun beat down on his naked back, and he fantasized he could feel the skin beginning to grow taut, then popping and curling loose in strips. There wasn't much water in the canteen, but he poured some on his back to ease the blistering pain.

Each valley promised to be the last, and each time, as the chestnut climbed to the top of a ridge, Slocum looked down expectantly, hoping to see the blue-green meander of Bracken's Creek, but each time he was disappointed. After a while, he started to imagine it was there anyway, and he'd feel a surge of energy shoot through him, only to fizzle out as the chestnut reached the valley floor and started up the next hill.

It was almost sundown when his eyes finally convinced him that this time they were seeing clearly. He let the horse make its way down through the grass, hanging on with the last of his strength. His arm throbbed incessantly, as if some small blacksmith sat on his shoulder, hammer in hand, and pounded away with every stride of the chestnut stallion.

The work crew spotted him, and he saw several of the men come running toward him, even Cookie, his suspenders flapping as he stumbled uphill through the tall grass.

Ben Donaldson got there first, lifted him from the saddle and took Slocum's full weight on his shoulders, then lowered him to the ground.

"Hitch a team," he shouted, then knelt beside the wounded man. "Slocum! Johnny, can you hear me? What happened, boy?"

Slocum tried to tell him, felt his lips move and the skin crack as the words tried to come out, but somehow he couldn't make himself understood.

"Get water, somebody," Donaldson said. Slocum could hear the words but they sounded as if they had come from a long way away, and they echoed, as if the speaker were in a long tunnel. He recognized Cookie as the old man bent over him, a pail of water in one hand, a dipper in the other. Cookie set the pail down and Slocum turned toward it, reaching out with his good arm, but Cookie pushed him back.

"Stay there, Johnny," the old man said, then brought the dipper to Slocum's lips. "Not much now, you hear? Take it a little at a time."

Slocum heard the creak of a wagon bed, and the hiss of its wheels in the grass, as it lumbered toward him. Cookie gave him another drink, then untied the sleeve binding the wound. The old man pursed his lips in a silent whistle, then stuck the tip of his tongue out between his teeth. "Not real bad. He just lost a lot of blood, looks like. We got to get him to town."

"Never mind that," Donaldson snapped. "We'll take him to the Double Deuce. Send Lyle to town and tell him to get Doc Andrews to hotfoot it out."

"What in the hell happened, do you think?" Cookie asked. When nobody volunteered an answer, he offered the dipper once more. The wagon had stopped, and Slocum could see its bulk just a few feet behind his head. It looked odd from that angle. He was looking up at the bottom of the wagon bed, and the brake handle seemed as tall as a lodgepole, towering over the seat. The jingle of the traces testified to the team's impatience.

Slocum closed his eyes, felt hands slip under him and he started to rise, as if he were floating. He could no longer feel the hands hoisting him up, and then he started to fly. Someone grunted, then Slocum's arm hit the side of the wagon and he blacked out.

When he came to, he was wrapped in a woolen blanket, the hard boards of the wagon bed cushioned by another beneath him. Somebody whose face he couldn't see in the twilight sat behind him, trying to keep him from rolling as the wagon pitched and tossed like a toy boat on a flood as it wound up a steep slope.

There was a slice of moon, not much more than a faint smile, floating against the deep blue. The stars would be out soon, he thought. It was a warm night. His skin felt hot, especially his face, and he wondered if he were fevered, maybe from an infection, then guessed it must still be the loss of blood affecting him. It was too soon for infection to have set in.

Or was it? He was no longer sure of time. He knew he would make it, knew that the worst was over, that he had enough strength, enough will to hang on until they reached the Double Deuce. But he'd never felt this weak before. It made him angry to feel so vulnerable, and already he was starting to feel stupid, as if he had made some tyro's mistake when he should have known better. The mistake had cost him, almost cost him his life, in fact, but he would set that right. As soon as he could get back in the saddle.

Slocum kept fading in and out of consciousness. Twice he came to and thought the wagon had stopped, only to feel it lurch beneath him. The third time, it ground slowly to a halt. Now he could see light spilling from the second-story windows of Mr. McCrae's house.

Then he smelled flowers, and a woman bent over him as he was lifted from the wagon. She was young, he thought, and so pretty.

And he was out again.

5

Slocum slept fitfully through the night. Each time he woke, he felt the throbbing of his arm and he imagined himself back in the saddle, hanging on for all he was worth. It felt as if the bed were moving beneath him. He could feel his heart hammering in his chest, and his thirst seemed unquenchable.

Once, he woke himself with his own moaning, and he saw the door open. A figure glided toward him, but it was too dark to see who it was and his eyes refused to focus well. He felt a hand on his forehead, the skin cool and smooth, and he wondered if it was the young woman he had seen for so brief a time when they lifted him from the wagon. A hand lifted his head, and a tumbler of water was pressed to his lips. He tried to drink, felt the water trickle from the corners of his mouth and, even though it was too dark for his nurse to see, he felt a slight twinge of embarrassment.

He gulped at the glass, swallowed several sips of water, then felt the hand withdraw and heard his attendant close the door again. He tried to say thank you, but his voice was an unintelligible croak in his mouth.

The next time he woke, the room was gray. He turned his head and saw the window. Its curtains were pulled closed, but were so gauzy they couldn't keep out the rising light. He felt better. His arm still ached, but his senses were under control now. When he rolled his head from side to side on the pillow, the furniture stayed put, and the room didn't start to spin.

He tried to sit up, but he was too weak. He lay there for a long time, running over the events of the previous day moment by moment, trying to find the missing pieces, as if it were a puzzle he hadn't quite gotten right. There had to be something he should have seen but had missed, some mistake he'd made that had almost cost him his life.

It was easy to say simply going into the canyon alone was his mistake, but he had the feeling his mistake had happened before that, he just didn't know what it was.

A small clock attracted his attention, its ticking finally drawing his eyes. It sat on a night table beside the bed. He glanced at it, waited for his eyes to focus on the slender hands, and saw that it was six thirty. So far, there hadn't been a sound from anywhere in the house, as if he were the only one in it.

Slocum swung his legs over the bed and reached for the floor with his bare feet. When he found it, he tried to sit up, using his legs to support his effort, but he was too drained. He just lay there, half in and half out of bed. He realized then that he was wearing a cotton nightshirt he'd never seen before. It certainly wasn't his.

It took him a long time to get back in the bed, and when he finally managed, he was exhausted. He closed his eyes again, and when they reopened, it was almost eight. The door was open, and he heard voices in the hall, whispering.

A moment later, Dan McCrae appeared in the doorway, with Ben Donaldson standing behind him and peering at Slocum over the smaller man's shoulder.

Slocum tried to smile, but it slid off his face before it had fully formed. "How you feeling, John?" McCrae asked. "How's the arm?"

Slocum nodded, licked his parched lips with a tongue like a razor strop. "All right, I guess," he croaked. "It's still there, anyway."

"Don't laugh, son, you come mighty close to losing more than that wing. What happened?"

Slocum swallowed hard, and Donaldson said, "You want some water, John?" Without waiting for an answer, he slipped past his boss and walked to the night table, poured water from a pitcher into a glass, and held it to Slocum's lips. The water was cool, and Slocum glanced instinctively at the pitcher, where he noticed beads of condensation trickling down its curved sides. He sipped greedily, and Donaldson patiently held the glass until Slocum nodded that he was finished.

Setting the glass down, Donaldson sat on the foot of the bed. McCrae crossed the room, spun a chair toward the bed, and sat down with the chair's back in front of him, propped his forearms on the polished wood, and smiled.

"You're gonna be just fine, John. Doc Andrews says you lost a hell of a lot of blood. It'll take you some time to get your strength back, but I don't want you to worry about anything. Your job'll be waiting for you, soon as you want it, but there's no rush. Doc says you'll probably be up and around in three or four days, but from the look of that arm, you won't be in no big rush to be driving fence posts."

"I always pull my own weight, Mr. McCrae. I don't need charity."

"John, about the only thing you're in any shape to pull is a long face. And as far as I'm concerned, it ain't charity. You was workin' for me when you got shot. I ain't about to turn my back on a man who was earning his pay. I don't know what the hell went on out there, but if Ben hadn't sent you, you wouldn'ta been there, so it just seems fair that you get paid for it. When you're up to it, you can stay on or leave, just as you like. But until then, you're on the payroll, same as everybody else around here." McCrae raised a cautionary finger, "And don't even think about arguing with me, John. The shape you're in, even an old man like me can whip you."

Slocum sighed. "Thank you, Mr. McCrae. And it's not that I'm not grateful. I don't want you to think that. It's just—"

"I know exactly what it is," McCrae interrupted. "I was like that once. Any young man worth his salt is, but fair's fair. That's all I'm sayin'. You put your shoulder to my wheel, seems like the grease ought to be on my tab. Now, you feel like talkin' a little bit about what happened?"

Slocum reached out for the pitcher, but McCrae beat him to it, topped off the glass, and held it out until Slocum was able to grip it securely. After taking a couple of sips, he lowered the glass to his chest and let his fingers slide down its sides to rest against his breastbone. "There's not much to tell, really."

"Where'd it happen, John?"

"Not too sure of names. Don't know the territory all that well. It was about twenty, maybe twenty-five miles from the work detail. A box canyon. Nothing special about it, I guess, except maybe for the waterfall."

"Inside," Donaldson asked, "hundred foot or so high, falls on a big rock before it runs out the length of the canyon?"

Slocum nodded. "Sounds right."

"I know the place. Most folks around here call it Rock Falls Canyon. Not too imaginative, but I guess if it lets you find the place, it don't have to be. Anyhow, go on, John. That where it happened?"

Slocum took a deep breath. "Yeah, I was on my way out, actually. Found a campsite in the canyon, but it was old. The ashes were cold, and it didn't look like anybody was planning on coming back anytime soon, so I headed out. Stopped to get a drink," and here he took another pull on the tumbler. Swallowing the cool water brought it all back very clearly, and he puffed out his cheeks and blew his breath out in a tight stream before continuing. "I was lucky, I guess. Could have killed me, for sure, if he'd been a better shot."

"You get a look at him?"

"Never did. Don't even know for sure it was the man I followed from Bracken's Creek. If I had to bet on it, I'd say it was, but I couldn't prove it."

"You see the shooter at Bracken's Creek?"

Slocum shook his head.

Donaldson said, "I got closer than anybody, Dan, and there wasn't nothing to see. He was pretty near the far side of the valley by the time I come over the ridge. With field glasses, maybe I could have seen something to hang a hat on, but . . ."

"Anything else, John?"

Slocum shook his head again. "The only thing strange, what I've been wondering off and on since it happened, though . . ." He paused, and McCrae leaned forward, waiting for the end of the thought. "Well, I wonder how come he didn't finish me off. That's what makes me think it's probably the same man. Shooting cows isn't like shooting a man. Even if it's long range, and you shoot him in the back, you know what you're doing. I'd bet the man isn't a killer."

"He shot you, didn't he?"

"Maybe it was an accident. Maybe he just wanted to scare me off. He only hit me once. Maybe he shaved it a little close."

Donaldson shook his head. "More likely he's a lousy shot, and just couldn't nail you. I'd bet my hat that's what it was. Don't you be making this guy out to be some softhearted sheepherder who wouldn't hurt a fly. He damn near killed you."

"But we don't know that it was a sheepherder, softhearted or otherwise," Slocum said.

"I know that," Donaldson snapped. "But what the hell else could it be? No reason to shoot cows unless you want to get rid of the man who owns 'em. The only folks around here fit that suit of clothes smell like mutton to me."

"You're probably right, Ben," McCrae said, "but I don't want you goin' off half-cocked. We don't know anything for sure, and I sure as hell do not—and I can't state this strongly enough—do not want the boys getting into a shootin' war with them damn sheepdippers. I'm holdin' you responsible for that. Anybody's got any other idea, you set him straight, and if he don't like it, you hand him his walkin' papers. I won't have it."

Donaldson looked dubious, but he nodded. "I know what you're saying, Mr. McCrae, but if them sheep men start shooting, I can't ask the boys to sit there like ducks on a pond. They pack pistols, and they'll use 'em if they need to."

"That's different," McCrae said, bobbing his head. "I understand that. I don't want the men to get hurt, but I don't want them starting anything either. That's all I'm saying. We got enough trouble, what with that regulator the Cattleman's Association brought in."

He stood up then, and said, "Doc Andrews will be by later, John, to take a look at you. He left some medicine for you to ease the pain in the meantime. And he left some orders about your meals, too. You'll be eatin' pretty well for the next few days, try to build your blood back up."

"I appreciate it, Mr. McCrae."

"Don't thank me, till you get through it, John. My daughter Samantha'll be looking after you, and she don't take 'no' too kindly. She'll be riding herd on you the way her mother would have if she were still with us. You'll probably cry uncle before the day's out, but you listen to her. She knows what she's doing." And with a laugh, he added, "Besides, you can't hardly get up and run away from her, so if you don't want to spend a week trussed up like a Christmas turkey, you better do like she says. You want anything, you tell Samantha and she'll see you get it."

McCrae turned to go, then stopped in the doorway. "One more thing, John."

"Mr. McCrae?"

"Don't hold out on me, John. If you know more than you're tellin' because you have some idea of gettin' even soon as you're able, you forget about it. The law will handle it, all right? Merrill Hansen's our sheriff, and he's a good man. Not to mention a friend of mine. He comes by to ask you a few questions—which I'm sure he will—you tell him what he wants to know."

"I'm not holding anything back," Slocum bristled.

McCrae bobbed his head. "See that you don't, John. See that you don't."

6

Slocum was already getting bored. Not used to being idle, he felt as if he had been accused of some crime he had forgotten, then tried and sentenced to life. Trying to imagine what it would be like to be confined in a jail cell, the closest he could come was his present situation. He knew the arm would trouble him for a few days, but a few days was a few too many. He wanted to be up and around, *doing* something, anything, just so he didn't feel like he was on a leash.

He heard someone on the stairs and tried to sit up. Suddenly a tray appeared in the doorway, almost as if it were floating there on its own. Then it started to move again, and its bearer came into view. She took his breath away. Nearly six feet tall, with the blackest, longest hair he'd ever seen, she gave him a smile that would melt a glacier. "Feeling hungry?" she asked.

Slocum was speechless. He nodded, felt foolish, and fumbled for a couple of words that were all but lost in his stupor. All he could do was bob his head up and down.

41

"Cat got your tongue?" She smiled again as she crossed the room, the tray balanced on the fingertips of her left hand. With her right, she spun the chair McCrae had left beside the bed, then lowered the tray to it. The coffee was lapping at the rim of the cup, but only a drop or two made it out of the china to dribble down into the saucer.

"I didn't make this, so I can't vouch for how good it is," she said.

"You're Miss McCrae, I gather?"

That smile again, this time lingering a moment. She nodded. "Daddy told you I'd be looking after you, I guess?"

"Yes, he did," Slocum croaked. "But . . ." he stopped, uncertain what to say next.

"But he didn't tell you I was so tall, did he?"

That wasn't it either, but Slocum had to say something, so he mumbled, "He didn't tell me your name," he lied, and knew that she knew it.

"He didn't tell me yours, either," she said, grinning to let him know she was as adept at prevarication as he was, "but I know what it is. John, right?"

"Yes."

"Mine's Samantha, but you can call me Sam. I've always been a tomboy, so the name is a blessing, even though I hate it."

"It's a lovely name, Miss McCrae."

"I told you you could call me Sam. Why don't you, unless you want to aggravate me . . . ?" She made a fist and waved it threateningly.

"No, of course not, Sam. I sure don't want to aggravate you."

She sat on the edge of the bed after smoothing the cover. "Can you sit up or would you like me to feed you?"

Slocum shook his head. "I can sit up, I think."

"You're sure? Don't do it just because men are supposed to be able to sit up when they're half dead. I don't care much about that sort of thing. It won't impress me in the least, John."

"No, really, I can sit up."

She folded her arms then and watched as he raised himself on the elbow of his good arm. The movement twisted his upper body, and the torsion sent a screaming hornet tearing through his left arm. He winced, bit his tongue, and shook his head, trying to dislodge the tears forming in the corners of his eyes.

Samantha laughed. "So, you're just like all the others, aren't you, John?"

"How's that?" he said, clenching his teeth as he maneuvered on the bed until he was close enough to the edge to reach over for the coffee. The movement brought his thigh into contact with her left hip. Despite the layers of cloth, he thought he could feel the heat of her body, decided it couldn't be, and let his thigh stay where it was. Samantha didn't seem to mind.

"How's that? Well, let me see, where shall I start? Would you like the list in alphabetical order?"

"Why not?" He smiled, and she grinned at him mischievously. "All right, here goes: a is for arrogant, b is for buffoonish, c is for conniving, d is for—"

Slocum threw up his hands in mock surrender. Like the previous movement, it made his left arm hurt like hell, but he ignored the pain long enough to say, "Okay, okay, I see what you mean. But I'm not like that."

"Of course you're not. But just in case you were wondering, the d was for deceitful." She smiled triumphantly, and Slocum lay back on the pillow.

"Just teasing you, Mr. Slocum," she said. "I know the wound must be very painful. Why don't you let me feed you. It won't hurt you in a day or so. When you're feeling better, you'll be on your own. You won't forget how to use a fork in two or three days, will you?" He started to shake his head in the negative, but she continued. "You do know how to use one, don't you?"

Slocum laughed outright. "Yeah, I do. I just never know which one is for the salad when there are two."

"Ah, a man of some breeding, I see. Judging by your accent, you must have come by it legitimately. Atlanta, maybe, or Savannah."

"Close."

"Close enough?" She wriggled on the bed, and once more he became aware of the pressure of her hip against his thigh.

"I see you have several ways to tease a man," he said.

"Why, suh, I do believe you've impugned mah virtue."

"Never, Miss McCrae. You do have virtue, don't you?"

"Touché, Mr. Slocum."

"You didn't answer my question, Miss McCrae."

"Nor will I, Mr. Slocum."

Slocum realized now that he was not about to get the upper hand, and he decided to let Samantha McCrae have her way. She picked up the fork and used it to cut the strips of bacon into smaller pieces, and he used the time to study her.

Her eyes were coal black, her lips full, and seemed to be pouting when her face was at rest. Her skin was tan, as if she spent a great deal of time outdoors, so different from the women she had so neatly parodied with her southern drawl. And unlike those women she made no effort to conceal the dusting of freckles on her turned-up nose. But it was her figure that was most impressive. Despite her height, she was anything but a scarecrow. Full breasts were made to seem even more so by the narrow waist. Her legs were long, and well muscled, her thighs stretching the faded denim of her jeans taut. Her hips were broad, but not enough to suggest that she would someday waddle under added weight. He could imagine what she looked like naked, and the thought was not at all unpleasant.

She turned suddenly and caught him scrutinizing her. She blushed the least little bit, as if she guessed what he was thinking. But she didn't seem to mind. Instead, she hoisted some egg on the fork and said, "Open wide, Johnny." Bringing the food to his mouth, she said, "I'll make a choo-choo noise, if you like."

Slocum shook his head, nearly knocking the egg from the fork. "No, thanks," he said. "I think I can manage to eat without it."

She shoveled the food into his mouth rapidly, barely giving him time to breathe between forkfuls. He hadn't realized how hungry he had been, but he kept up with her, and the food, despite her insinuations as to its dubious taste, was excellent. When the bacon, eggs and fried potatoes were gone, she split a biscuit for him, poured a little honey from a cruet on the inner sides, and held one half up for him to nibble on. Some of the honey dribbled down his chin, and she reached out with a fingertip to wipe it away, then licked her finger clean. "Too good to waste," she said.

"I was thinking the same thing," Slocum said.

"Don't trouble yourself to construct clever sexual innuendoes, Mr. Slocum. I believe in plain speaking. I know it's not supposed to be ladylike, but I don't give a good Goddamn about that. I grew up on this ranch, and I've been to school in the east, so I've seen nature in its rawest form and dueled with the most rapacious of your eastern predators."

She seemed pleased with her pronouncement, and straightened a little to await his reply.

"I just meant the honey was very good," he said.

"Of course you did. I knew that. I was just trying to see whether your vocabulary was larger than that of the average Wyoming steer. Apparently it is. That's good."

"Why is that, Miss McCrae?"

"Because I get very tired of talking to sweaty men about the weather and the price of beef in Chicago. Since my mother died, I rarely get to discuss anything else."

"How long since . . ."

"Two years." She looked away then, and Slocum reached out to pat her on the shoulder. She flinched when he touched her, and he thought for a moment she was going to get up off the bed, but she just shivered for a second, shook her head, and turned back to him. "Sorry. I still miss her, I guess."

"You always will, Samantha. And there's nothing wrong with that." He was really talking about himself, and she seemed to realize it.

"When did your mother die?"

"During the war."

"You weren't home, were you?"

"No, I wasn't. How did you know that?"

"Because it's the things we don't get to do that make us realize how fragile the family is. If you had been there, you would feel differently, as if you had done what you could. But when you're a thousand miles away, you blame yourself, for things you should have said, for things you might have done that could have made a difference. I don't mean saved their lives or anything like that, just, you know, tied up the loose ends a little. The way a final chord resolves a musical composition. When it's missing, something is not right, and you sense it, even if you can't explain it."

"I guess."

"Don't be afraid to agree with me, Mr. Slocum. Women are often right, you know."

Slocum nodded. "It's not that. I guess I just didn't realize how much it mattered to me that I wasn't home when mother died. I've never talked about it before."

"Not even with your family?"

It was Slocum's turn to choke back an unpleasant memory. "No, not even with my family," he said. They had all been dead when he came home from the war, but that was more than he cared to share, even with so striking a woman as Samantha McCrae.

She sensed that he wanted to change the subject, and she accommodated him. "Would like some more to eat? There's plenty of bacon and potatoes left. I can break a few eggs if I have to."

Slocum laughed. "I'll just bet you can," he said. "But, no, I'm fine."

She stood up then, and the place where her hip had pressed against him felt suddenly empty. Abruptly, she leaned over and kissed him on the forehead. "Don't read anything into that," she said, grinning. "You just remind me of the brother I never wanted. I'll be back later, when Doc Andrews gets here to check you out."

"Do you mean you'll check me out, or the doctor will?"

"We'll see," she said, turning to go. He watched her leave, enjoying the play of muscles in her long legs. Then he closed his eyes to dream a little.

7

The days hung around him like buzzards, but Slocum could feel his strength returning. And every time Samantha paid him a visit, he could feel his spirits rise a little. When she'd gone, they settled down, but never as low as they had been before her appearance. She continued to tease him, and even to feed him sometimes. His arm was healing rapidly, but he enjoyed her company, and didn't want to break the spell, so he took it easy.

In the long hours of solitude, though, he flexed the arm, biting into his lower lip to keep from crying out the first day, the second permitting himself a soft moan, and by the third, it still hurt, but was nothing he couldn't handle.

The doctor came twice, changed the dressing on the wound, and pronounced it as progressing nicely each time. He was drinking a lot of fluid, coffee and water mostly, but once a day, Samantha brought him a large bowl of thick broth, usually chicken, which she claimed the doctor had ordered for him.

But while time seemed to stand still inside his room,

outside things were changing rapidly, and each little scrap of news made him that much more anxious to get back on his feet. Two more small groups of dead steers had been found, both, just like the first two, felled by a single shot to the head. That would have been bad enough, but there was every sign that the troubles were beginning to escalate. More than a dozen sheep had been slaughtered but, unlike the steers, their throats had been slit, and there was no reason to believe that it was anything but retaliation.

On the morning of the fourth day, Dan McCrae paid him another visit, while Samantha hovered in the background. "How you feeling, John?" McCrae asked.

"Coming along. Should be up and around in a day or two. Ready for work in a week or so."

"Light duty, John. You won't be up to more than that for a couple of weeks. Maybe three. That's what Doc Andrews says, anyhow."

"Doctors always make things seem worse than they are. That way, if you get well quicker, they can take credit for it."

McCrae laughed. "I thought you were new around here, but it sounds to me like you got Doc's number. Right on the money. He's a good man, though, and you couldn't ask for a better doctor."

"Oh, I like him fine. It's just that I'm starting to feel like a prisoner here."

McCrae nodded. "You have the run of the house, John. You want to go down and sit in the study, feel free. Hell, maybe you could sit out on the porch, if you feel up to it. Just don't overdo it, that's all. Samantha will keep an eye on you. I can have one of the boys help get you down the steps, if you need it."

Slocum shook his head. "Thanks, Mr. McCrae, but I can handle things fine. As long as I take it slow, I'll be all right."

McCrae nodded. Then, looking over his shoulder at Samantha, he asked, "Would you mind leaving us alone for a few minutes, Sam?"

"Secrets, Daddy?"

"No secrets, honey. But there's some things you don't need to know."

"Same thing, it sounds like to me," Samantha said.

"Well, still, would you mind?"

"Not if you insist."

"Then I do, Sam. I'm sorry, but . . ."

"No need to be sorry, Daddy. I saw the way you kept things from mother. I guess I'm used to it."

"Sam . . ."

But she stalked out of the room, slamming the door behind her.

McCrae looked at Slocum and shrugged. "Damn girl's just like a filly. You can't get close enough to break her, and I don't know as I'd want to, anyhow."

"She's a strong-willed girl, that's for sure," Slocum agreed. "What did you want to talk about?"

"I guess you heard about the dead sheep?" He waited for Slocum to respond, and even when the wounded man nodded, he didn't continue immediately. Instead, he walked to the window and pulled the curtains aside. "Beautiful this time of year," he said. "I can see all the way to the Bitterroots when the light is right."

"You didn't come up here to tell me about the scenery, Mr. McCrae."

The rancher turned, but stayed at the window, lowering himself to the sill and draping the curtains around his shoulders to avoid wrinkling them. "No," he said, "I didn't come up here to talk about the scenery. I came to ask you a favor."

"Go ahead. I reckon I owe you, Mr. McCrae."

"No, John, you don't owe me a thing. I don't want you to think that. I don't want you to feel like you got to do what I'm about to ask, just because you work for me. I'm not that kind of man."

"Fair enough. Still, I owe you. What do you want me to do?"

"First, I got to give you some background. There's some things happening around here that I don't like. I'm not quite sure what I can do about them, but I feel like I got to try, before things get out of hand altogether. Some of the ranchers have gotten together to bring in a regulator, like I told you, a man named Cord Meyer. You heard of him?"

Slocum shook his head. "Can't say I have, no. But I know what a regulator is, and I know it means trouble."

"I agree with you, John. I never yet heard of a regulator who didn't have too easy a finger on the trigger, and I reckon Meyer is no different. The thing is, all the ranchers around here—the big cattle ranchers that is— are contributing to pay Meyer's fee and . . ."

"You one of the contributors, Mr. McCrae?"

The rancher was silent for a long time. He looked out the window again, his head disappearing behind the gauzy lace of the curtains. When he reappeared, he said, "Yes, I am, as a matter of fact. But not for the same reasons you might think. I figure the only way to keep things from spinning out of control is to know what's going on. If I didn't contribute, I'd be out in the cold. This way, I think maybe I can keep Meyer from starting a range war. If I'm lucky. But I can't do it alone."

"That's where the favor comes in, is it?"

McCrae nodded. "Yeah, it is."

"What do you want me to do?"

"Nothing much. Just keep your eyes open, keep me informed. The hands are likely to gossip among themselves, talk about things they wouldn't tell me."

"You want me to spy, is that it?"

"Look, John, I told you you could say no. I'll understand if you do, but . . . I don't really have much choice, even though you do. Ben Donaldson won't do it, but the hands don't tell him much anyhow. They think he's too close to me. They're good men, all of 'em, but you know how things are. Hands sometimes think they know better than the men they work for. I suppose you've felt like that from time to time."

"Yeah, I have. Not often, but often enough to know what you're talking about."

"Well, I want to know what's behind those dead sheep. I know Ray Dalton, the man they belonged to, and he's a bit of a hothead, so I want to head off trouble before it gets started, if I can. And I don't want the boys following Meyer's lead, because I know what can happen if they do."

"Who killed the sheep, Mr. McCrae?"

"I don't know. It could be anybody. There must be twenty ranches around here. Figure an average of twenty hands or so, and you got close to four hundred men, any one of who could have done it."

"Plus the owners of those ranches," Slocum said.

McCrae looked at him sharply. He seemed to tense up for a moment, then took a deep breath and relaxed. "Yeah, them too, John. Them too."

"And Meyer."

McCrae nodded, slowly. "And Meyer," he said. "It's the kind of thing he might do. I've done some checking, and I don't much like what I hear. He's a bit of a hothead himself. Likes to stir up trouble, because it makes his job harder and his pockets fuller. The more trouble there is, the longer he stays around and the more money hc makes. I don't know that that's what's happening here, because he's only been around a couple of weeks or so, but. . . . Anyhow, I'm still tryin' to track down more information on him."

"You think maybe he killed the beeves?"

"Why would he do that? He's working for us. Why kill our stock?"

"Like you said: the more trouble there is, the more money he makes."

"But that'd be awful soon, don't you think? I mean we found the first ones just five days ago."

"Meyer was already here, wasn't he?"

"Yeah, he was, but—"

"And there wasn't much trouble before that, was there? Just a lot of talk."

"First off, you got to understand that talk is trouble, if it's a certain kind of talk. What we were trying to do was make sure it stayed talk."

"So why was Meyer hired? What was he supposed to do? Intimidate the sheepherders?"

McCrae shrugged. "I guess so, yeah."

"And you don't think that could make things worse? You said Dalton is a hothead. In my experience, the best way to make trouble is to threaten somebody like Ray Dalton. He flies off the handle, picks up a gun, then you got exactly what you were trying to avoid. And you have to remember one thing about Cord Meyer—it might be the first time you hired a regulator, but he's been in the business a while. He can pick up the lay of the land real quick, see things you don't, and use them to his own advantage before you realize what's happened."

"Look, John, I told you already, it wasn't my idea. But I went along so that I could keep a lid on things. Now, it looks like somebody blew the lid off. You know as well as I do that whoever tried to kill you had something to do with the dead cattle. No other explanation makes sense."

"But it probably wasn't Cord Meyer, because he'd hardly have missed me at that range. A man like him can hit a dime at three hundred yards. He'd never have missed me in that canyon. Once, maybe, but not more than that. Whoever tried to shoot me was not much of a marksman. So if Meyer was behind it, there's somebody in it with him, either one of the local hands, or somebody he brought in from outside."

"I don't understand what you're getting at. If it wasn't Meyer, then why does it matter that he's here?"

"Because when you get a bunch of men running around taking shots at other men, sooner or later somebody gets killed. It wasn't me this time, but it could have been. And you can bet your boots that the next time, or the time after that, it won't be a near miss."

"So . . ." McCrae said, "you'll do it, then?"

Knowing he was biting into a big loaf, Slocum nodded

slowly, "Yeah, I'll do it, Mr. McCrae."

"Good. Thank you."

"I just hope I know what I'm doing."

"So do I, John. So do I."

"Do me a favor, Mr. McCrae."

"What's that, John?"

"Don't bet the farm on it, all right?"

8

By Friday morning, it had been eight days since the shooting. Slocum had been getting around fairly well. His arm still hurt, and it wasn't ready for him to go back to work, but his strength was back. He was sitting on the rear gallery of the main house when Dan McCrae stepped out and thrust a long package wrapped in brown paper at him.

"What's this?" Slocum asked.

"Open it," McCrae said. His leathery face crinkled into a broad smile. His moustache twitched in expectation. He took off his hat and ran one bronzed hand across the thick white tangles of his hair and leaned back against the wall.

Slocum popped the brown string against the thick paper, then tugged it until it snapped. He set the broken strand on the floor beside his chair and shook the package. "Heavy," he said.

"You gonna open it or are you just gonna sit there and try to guess what it is?"

In answer, Slocum tore at the brown paper, starting

at one end. The printing on the carton inside told him everything he needed to know. It was a Winchester carbine. He ripped off the rest of the paper, opened the box, and lifted the cloth-wrapped carbine out, leaving the carton in his lap. Peeling the cloth back, he enjoyed the tang of gun oil, and when the gleaming new carbine had been revealed, he hefted it admiringly. The polished walnut stock shone in the sunlight almost as brightly as the blue steel of the barrel.

"It's beautiful," he said. "But . . ."

"No buts, John. That'll replace the one you left up in Rook Falls Canyon. I sent Dave Duncan up there to get it, but he couldn't find it. So . . ."

"I'll pay you back, Mr. McCrae."

"The hell you will. You already earned it." McCrae leaned toward the door and whistled. "Come on out, boys," he said.

Slocum jerked his head around in time to see Duncan, Ben Donaldson and about half a dozen more of the hands crowd through the door onto the gallery.

"What the hell?"

"We figured it was about time you bellied up to a real bar and downed a little bourbon, someplace smokey, that smelled of sweat and spit and where the women wore a little too much powder and not enough clothes," Donaldson announced. "You up to it?"

Slocum laughed out loud. "Damn right," he said. "Let's go. That is, if I can get an advance on my pay." He glanced at McCrae, but the rancher shook his head, his face suddenly stony and impassive.

"No way in hell," McCrae said. "I don't pay people to drink liquor, Slocum."

Donaldson leaned over and clapped Slocum on the back. "He's just funnin' with you, John. The drinks are on Mr. McCrae," he said. "Long as you don't have a hollow leg."

"Hollow head, maybe, but my legs are sound," Slocum said, grinning. He got out of the chair and reached out to take McCrae's extended hand. "Thanks, Mr. McCrae," he said. "I really appreciate it."

"You just come back sober, son. You got a lot of work around here, and you damn well better grab an oar." But McCrae was laughing, and Slocum could only shake his head.

"Go on and get ready," Donaldson told him. "Sprinkle a little flower water on yourself, so the ladies'll treat you kindly, and we'll meet you out front in about fifteen minutes."

"Deal," Slocum said. He bent to retrieve the discarded wrapping, but McCrae stepped on the paper. "Leave it, John. I'll take care of it. You go on and git ready."

Nodding his thanks, Slocum parted the knot of cowhands and walked quickly. His arm hurt a little with the unaccustomed exertion, but everything else felt fine.

In his room, he took off his shirt, eyed the bandages warily, then gave his face a quick rinse. He leaned forward to cheek his face in a shaving mirror. Running his hands over his cheeks, he felt a little stubble, but decided it didn't matter.

"You look just fine."

He spun around to see Samantha leaning against the inside of the doorframe. Her long legs were crossed casually, and her arms were folded under her breasts. "Going to find a woman, are you?" she asked.

"No, not at all," Slocum spluttered. "Just . . ."

"That's not what I hear."

"Oh, well, they were just teasing me, that's all."

He reached for a fresh shirt, swung it across his shoulders and worked at getting both arms in the sleeves. It was a simple movement, one he'd done ten thousand times, but it suddenly seemed very complicated, even difficult, as the wounded arm bent and flexed and swelled with waves of pain.

When he finally had the shirt on, he buttoned it quickly, then turned around. But Samantha was gone.

He moved quickly down the hall, buckling on his gunbelt. He passed an open door, and glanced through.

Samantha was sitting on a sofa, a book in her lap. "Be careful," she said. "And don't have too good a time."

"No danger of that," Slocum said.

"I hope not." She opened the book then, without giving him another glance. He felt a little silly standing there, then shrugged and started down the hall again, calling over his shoulder, "Good-bye, Miss McCrae."

If she heard him, she didn't answer.

The hands were waiting out front, already in the saddle. Slocum's chestnut was saddled and ready. He mounted up and Donaldson told him to take the point. "It's your party," he said, "so you might as well get there first. You get the pick of the booze and the ladies that way."

They all bantered with him on the ride into Bracken, most of the time insulting him good-naturedly, making comments about his eyesight, his trail sense, and, especially, his reluctance to put in a good day's work. Dave Duncan wondered whether it was worth getting shot to get out of running fence, and Slocum took a swipe at him, knocking Duncan's hat off, which was promptly squashed by Donaldson's horse.

"That hat should have been retired a long time ago, Davey," Donaldson said.

Bracken was a small town. It depended on the surrounding ranches for its survival and, like most cow towns, it was long on saloons and short on just about everything else. The Double Deuce hands favored a place called the Red Sombrero that was operated by a transplanted Texan. The women tended to dark-haired señoritas, and the Mexican decor made the place seem exotic by Bracken standards.

Inside, a game of faro was already in progress in one corner, despite the early hour, and nearly a dozen men were strung along the battle-scarred bar, while a handful of others sat in twos and threes at bare round tables, cards spread out among the chips and half-empty glasses.

As the Double Deuce hands walked in, the patrons stopped what they were doing just long enough to see whether they recognized the newcomers. Donaldson called to the bartender for drinks all around, as the hands pulled a couple of tables together, and Duncan broke out a fresh deck of cards.

"Got to win myself enough for a new hat," he said, laughing as he shuffled the stiff cards.

"Hell, Dunc, you ought to pay Slocum for getting rid of the other one," Doak Henry said.

A waitress came over to take their drink orders, and Duncan pulled her down onto his lap, sliding his chair back to make room for her. When the orders were taken, she tried to get up, and when Duncan wouldn't let her rise, she started to get annoyed. Duncan scowled, cupped her breasts in his thick-fingered hands, and said, "Honey, you ought to be stayin' right here. You can just yell out the order. I don't think I want to let these beauties go just yet."

She wriggled a bit, trying to pull free, but Duncan was adamant. She turned to him, gave him a big smile, and leaned toward him, her lips puckered. "That's more like it, honey," he said, closing his eyes and waiting for the promised kiss. The waitress leaned closer, took his lower lip in her teeth and bit down just hard enough to make her point. Duncan yelped and let go of her and she sprang from his lap as the other hands cheered.

Duncan was angry, reached for her and caught her by the skirt. Slocum reached across the table, took Duncan's arm in his right hand and squeezed. "Let her go, Dunc. It's too early in the morning for that."

Duncan glared at Slocum. "Hey, Slocum. You ain't in charge here. I don't give a damn about—"

"Slocum don't care, Dunc, 'cause he's pokin' Samantha some. So he don't know what it's like to need to scrape the fuzz off his antlers." Doak Henry laughed, but Duncan looked as if he'd been punched in the stomach. He looked at Slocum, his eyes almost yellow with bile.

Slocum squeezed a little harder, and Duncan let go of the fistful of brocade he had tangled in his fingers.

"Boys, let's not get out of hand just yet," Donaldson cautioned. The waitress took advantage of the opportunity to make her escape and deliver the drink order. When they were delivered, the bartender brought them over on a tray. "You want to pull my skirt?" he asked, dropping Duncan's whiskey on the table with a crack.

Duncan frowned but said nothing.

The drinks kept coming, and within an hour, most of the hands were three sheets to the wind. Slocum drank quietly, husbanding a bourbon, sipping it occasionally, and joining in the raillery only when it couldn't be avoided. But Duncan sulked. He drank rapidly, tossing his whiskey down in one or two gulps, and staring at the wall rather than joining in the fun. The others ignored him, as if they were used to his sullenness.

"Something bothering you, John?" Donaldson asked, leaning over to whisper the question.

Slocum shook his head. "Nope. Just trying to get used to things again, I guess."

"Don't let Duncan get under your skin. He's a good fellow. Just a little green around women. He thinks you got to treat them like livestock to make them notice him. He'll learn."

Slocum nodded. "I just thought he was a little rough on the girl."

"He was, you're right. But she's in a rough business, just like he is. I'd bet a week's pay she could have handled him. Them Mexican gals got a lot of spirit, you know. They seen a lot worse than Dave Duncan."

Some of the hands were playing poker, and the noise had dwindled to an occasional call for another drink, the click of chips and the slap of cards on the hard wooden tables.

It was a different kind of silence than that Slocum had endured for the past week, and it felt good to be sitting there. He was more than willing to forget about Duncan's rudeness.

"I guess I'm just a little tense, is all," he said.

"Hell, John, have another drink. Try to relax some. This is supposed to be fun."

Slocum nodded, reaching for the bourbon. The door banged open, and Ray Dalton stomped through, meandering toward the bar in a rather uncertain stride.

"Fucking sheepdipper," Duncan said, getting to his feet. "Time to take care of this bullshit."

He started toward the bar. "Dalton, come here."

Ray Dalton turned around, tilted his head back, then pushed his hat back on his forehead. "You talking to me, cowboy?"

Duncan's chair fell to the floor as he moved away from the table. The crack of wood on wood silenced the barroom as efficiently as the crack of a judge's gavel.

"You bet I am," Duncan answered.

9

Duncan moved a step toward the drunken sheepherder.

"Sit down, Davey," Donaldson barked. He kicked the chair out behind him and moved around the table toward the cowhand. Duncan let his eyes drift toward Donaldson, just a quick flick, then fixed them on Dalton again.

"Sumbitch been killin' our steers," Duncan hissed.

Dalton grinned at him. "I heard about that. Fact is, there's a bunch more dead cows out there this morning. Why in hell you think I'm here celebratin'? But I didn't kill 'em. I'd like to buy a drink for the man who done it, though."

"You're lying through your teeth, Dalton. It was you or one of them other sheepdippin' bastards who done it. You're all alike, so it don't make no difference to me whether you—"

Donaldson grabbed Duncan by the shoulder and spun him around. The burly foreman stuck his fist under Duncan's nose. "You shut up and sit down, Davey, or, as God is my witness, I'll coldcock you." He let go of

Duncan's shoulder, and swept him back toward the table as easily as if he were a scarecrow full of straw.

To the sheepherder, he said, "You better find someplace else to drink, Dalton. I don't want no trouble, but we were here first and you're not welcome."

"It's a free country, Benjamin me lad," Dalton said, teetering the least little bit on his heels. "And in a free country a thirsty man can drink wherever the hell he wants to."

Tom Flanagan, the bartender, stepped out from behind the bar. He moved in behind Dalton, tapped him on the shoulder and, when Dalton turned, took him by the arm. Tugging the sheep man toward the bar, he said, "I'll give you one on the house, Ray, but then you'd best listen to Ben. Besides, Mr. Cardona don't want no trouble in here. It's not good for business."

Dalton turned to grin at Donaldson, his bloodshot eyes bulging a little. "You hear that, Benjamin? Mr. Flanagan is a real gentleman, he is. And he wants to buy me a drink. I believe I'll accept his gentlemanly offer." Dalton leaned on the bar then, slid along it looking for a stool with his hip and, when he found one, tried to sit on it. He misjudged, and the stool slid out from beneath him, sending him sprawling on the floor. He lay there a moment stunned, then started laughing.

The waitress who had narrowly avoided Duncan's meaty paws helped him to his feet, brushed the sawdust from Dalton's clothes, and helped him onto a stool. Then she turned and stared pointedly at Duncan, as if to challenge him to interfere.

"Just like a greaser bitch," Duncan muttered.

"Shut your mouth, Duncan," Slocum snapped.

"You know, Slocum, I'm startin' to think that whoever tried to plug your ass was doin' us a favor. Only we didn't know it. But I'm beginning to think maybe I'll take up a collection to pay him to finish the job."

Slocum stood up and grabbed Duncan by the front of his shirt. He jerked the drunken cowhand forward and leaned into his face. The smell of whiskey on Duncan's

breath nearly made Slocum gag, but he shook it off and
said through clenched teeth, "I've had about enough of
you today, Duncan. Maybe you should go on home and
sleep it off."

"Like the sheepdipper said, Slocum, it's a free country. And since Mr. McCrae is buyin' the drinks, I don't
reckon you have a whole hell of a lot to say about it,
now, do you?"

Slocum gave a jerk of his arm, let go without warning,
and Duncan fell to the floor. He lay there for a moment,
stunned, and Slocum turned back to his seat. "I think
maybe I better go, Ben," he said.

"Aw, forget about it, John. Dunc don't mean nothing.
He just don't hold his liquor too good, that's all."

Slocum nodded. "I know, but it seems like he's not
gonna be satisfied until somebody pushes his face in for
him. I'd just as soon it wasn't me."

"One more, and I'll haul his ass out of here myself,
John. Just relax."

Against his better judgment, Slocum agreed to stay.
After Donaldson ordered another round for himself and
Slocum, the doors opened again. Ray Dalton glanced
over his shoulder at the new arrival, then turned to prop
himself on the bar by the elbows. "Well, well, well," he
cackled, "if it ain't the famous regulator. You come in
to kill us all, did you, Mr. Regulator?"

The newcomer stared stonily at Dalton, glanced
around the saloon, then moved to the opposite end of
the bar.

"Who's that?" Slocum asked.

"That's Cord Meyer," Donaldson said. "The cattlemen
hired him to put some pressure on the sheepdippers. He's
lookin' into the stock killings, too. He's pure poison,
from what I hear. Mean as a snake. And he'd gut you
with that Bowie knife of his as soon as give you the
time of day."

Slocum said nothing. When the drinks arrived, he
eased his chair around to study Meyer in the mirror,
sipping at his whiskey with a thoughtful frown.

The man was thin as a rail, but looked wiry. He was over six feet tall, but couldn't have weighed more than a hundred seventy pounds, Slocum thought. He wore a pearl-handled Colt on his right hip, and a bone-handled Bowie knife in a beaded leather sheath on his left.

His boots were expensive, hand-tooled Mexican leather, with an elaborate design snaking up the heels and wrapping around to the insteps from either side. Black hair and blacker eyes made his face look pale, but the sun-bronzed color of his skin was noticeable against the light blue of a faded denim shirt.

Dalton, too, was studying the regulator, and downed the last of his drink and moved along the bar. "You got anything you want to say to me, Mr. Regulator?" Dalton said.

"I'm not in the habit of talking to sheepshit," Meyer said, watching Dalton in the murky glass over the bar.

"You ought to talk to me, though," Dalton said.

"Why's that?" Meyer still hadn't moved. He continued to stare hard at the mirror, and Dalton grinned at the glass, wobbling a little bit as he took a couple of steps toward Meyer.

The regulator turned around slowly. "You got something you want to say to me, you better say it and get your ass on out of here, sheepshit."

Dalton continued to grin. "You're a tough guy aren't you? So tough, you can sneak up on a sheep and cut its throat just as easy as you please. Isn't that right?"

"I wouldn't waste my time with no damn sheep. I wanted to cut something, I'd rather start with a sheepshit like you. I don't mind the animals, it's the bastards who own 'em are ruining this country."

"I figure that's bullshit. Tell me something, Mr. Regulator. When you killed them sheep, you fuck 'em first? Or afterwards?"

"I fuck anything in this shithole of a town, it'll be your wife."

"Now, that's plain nasty, Meyer. You want to step outside, talk about it a little?"

"We step outside, ain't but one of us comin' back in, mister. And it won't be you, I guarantee it."

Dalton took another step, stumbled and fell to his knees. He tottered for a moment, grasped at the air to try to regain his balance, but went on over. Meyer spat on the prostrate sheepherder, then brought his foot back and planted a vicious kick in Dalton's ribs.

Slocum heard the loud crack, and knew that a rib had broken, maybe two. He got to his feet, and Ben Donaldson grabbed his sleeve. "Don't mix in, John. This ain't our affair."

Slocum shook his head. "I won't sit here and watch him kick a drunken man to death."

He pulled free, and moved around the table. Meyer's eyes flicked toward him for a split second, then back to the prostrate Dalton. The regulator lashed out with his foot again, catching Dalton in the face. Once more, there was a loud crack, and Dalton rolled over on his back. His nose had been crushed, and blood spurted through both nostrils. His lower lip was torn, and blood seeped out of the corner of his mouth.

"You ought to leave him alone," Slocum said.

Meyer looked at him again. "Well, well, well, what have we got here? Another sheepshit, is it?"

Slocum ignored the jibe and continued across the floor. The woman who had been waiting on Slocum's table raised a hand to her face, shaking her head to warn him away, but Slocum smiled at her. "Don't worry about it, Señorita," he said. "Mr. Meyer was just leaving."

"The hell I was," Meyer said, easing away from the bar.

Slocum walked over to Dalton and dropped to one knee beside him. "You all right?" he asked.

Dalton mumbled something between his hands, which were cupped over his shattered face. Slocum leaned over and tried to pry the hands away, but Dalton turned his head and pulled free. "Leave me alone," he mumbled.

"You heard the man," Meyer said. "Why don't you just go on about your business, before you and me have a violent disagreement over somethin' that don't concern you."

Slocum straightened up. He reached into his pocket, pulled out a silver dollar, and tossed it to Tom Flanagan. "Give Mr. Meyer another drink, then he'll be leaving." The coin spun on the bar, rattled to a halt, and Flanagan reached out for it. But Meyer's right hand snaked out, grabbed Flanagan's wrist, and held on. "Leave the damn thing where it is. I don't want this man's drink. I can buy my own."

He slammed Flanagan's hand onto the bar, let go of the wrist, and took a step forward. Slocum tensed, feeling a twinge in his left arm. If Meyer pushed him, it would move quickly to gunplay, because Slocum was in no shape for a brawl.

Meyer saw the flinch and took it for a sign of weakness. He took another step. Then, almost too fast to see, he jerked the Bowie knife from its sheath and waved it under Slocum's nose. The squat, ugly blade caught orange light from the coal oil lamps, and looked almost as if it were made of beaten gold.

Meyer pressed forward, and Slocum took a step back. "You don't have too much to say now, do you, cowboy?"

"Put it up, Meyer," Slocum warned.

Meyer laughed. "Or what? What are you gonna do, cowboy? I can cut your throat before your gun clears the holster. And I've half a mind to do it anyhow."

Slocum took a deep breath, let it puff out his cheeks, then dropped to one knee, clearing his holster as the Bowie knife sliced the air just over his head. Slocum thumbed the hammer back, and Meyer froze. He nodded slowly, and then smiled. It was like looking at a cottonmouth. The lips curled, but the eyes stayed flat and black.

"You gonna use that?" Meyer asked.

"You bet your ass I am," Slocum said, waved the barrel, then squeezed the trigger. The bullet slammed into the Bowie knife, snapping the blade and sending both pieces clattering against the base of the bar.

Meyer shook his hand and cursed under his breath. He thought about going for his gun, but Slocum already had the hammer cocked.

To Flanagan, Slocum said, "I changed my mind, Tom. I don't want to buy this sonofabitch a drink after all. Give me back my dollar."

Flanagan snatched at the coin and tossed it to Slocum, who caught it in his left hand, then winced as he dropped the coin to the floor.

Meyer laughed. "Trouble with your arm, cowboy? I wonder why?"

"I got a feeling you already know," Slocum said. "But it won't make any difference. Get out of here."

Meyer turned to pick up the pieces of the Bowie knife, but Slocum snapped, "Leave it right there."

Meyer straightened slowly. Once more, his gunhand flexed, and Slocum thought for a split second that Meyer was going to be stupid enough to go for his gun. But the moment passed, and he started for the door. "See you again, cowboy," he said.

"Count on it," Slocum answered.

10

Slocum left the saloon by himself. He made the long ride back to the Double Deuce wondering whether he had made a mistake by confronting Cord Meyer. The regulator had a nasty streak—that much was obvious. And Ray Dalton was no prize either. But the sheepherder was a bad drinker, maybe even a nasty drunk, which was no crime. Meyer, on the other hand, was a killer. Nobody, Slocum thought, carries a Bowie knife on his hip unless he didn't mind getting a little blood on his hands.

He was wondering whether Dan McCrae had given him an impossible job, and whether McCrae even realized just how frayed tempers had become. The hostility Dave Duncan had demonstrated might be something personal. Maybe he couldn't handle his liquor, maybe he was just having a bad day; anything was possible. But there seemed to be more to it than that. And Duncan had seemed more than willing to go head to head with Slocum. That couldn't be explained as some simple conflict between cattlemen and sheepmen. It almost seemed as if the ordinarily affable Duncan suddenly had a personal grudge against him, Slocum thought. But there was no reason for it. At least none that Slocum could put his finger on.

By the time he reached the Double Deuce, he was tired. The trip had been a little more strain than he had anticipated. That was nobody's fault, but he didn't like the way it made him feel. Vulnerable was one thing, but the bad arm made him more than that; it made him reliant on his gun, and that was bound to lead to trouble. In more normal times, most arguments could be settled with words, some required the forceful application of knuckle to jawbone, and a very, very few could only be settled with cordite in the air. But the times were anything but normal, and, if that wasn't bad enough, he now had to go directly from words to bullets, and he didn't like it.

Riding down the long, winding, tree-lined lane leading to the main house of the Double Deuce, he wondered whether he ought to ask McCrae for his pay and pack his things. It might be best to move on. It wasn't that he was afraid, but a fresh start would give him time to mend, time to get a few things ironed out in his own mind, flatten a few wrinkles, and see just how much of the fabric of his life was in need of repair.

Slocum didn't take promises lightly, and he had promised Dan McCrae that he would keep his eyes open. But he hadn't promised to stay on the Double Deuce forever. McCrae was a reasonable man, and he would understand. The worst that might happen is McCrae would say no to the pay, and he'd leave with the same empty pockets he'd had when he arrived. There were worse things.

He had just about made up his mind when he rounded the last curve in the lane. The chestnut suddenly was splashed with brilliant sunlight, and he saw Sam McCrae and her father sitting on the front gallery.

McCrae waved and got out of his chair as Slocum rode up to the house. The rancher walked down the steps and met Slocum at the hitching post. "How'd it go?" he asked. "How come you're back so soon?"

Slocum grunted. "It didn't go well, Mr. McCrae. Not well at all. As a matter of fact, I was thinking of asking if you'd mind paying me through the end of the month."

McCrae looked confused. "I don't understand. I told Ben that I would pick up the bill in town."

"No, it's not that. I . . . well, to tell you the truth, I was thinking it might be best if I moved on."

"Moved on? But . . . why? I don't understand."

"Who's moving on?" Sam called, getting off the glider so quickly its chains rattled. She crossed the gallery and started down the stairs. "Who's leaving? John, are you leaving? You can't, you're not well enough."

Slocum gave her a wan smile, but addressed his answer to her father. "I had a little run-in with Cord Meyer this morning. Ray Dalton was there, too. It got ugly real quick. And I'm in no shape to be brawling in a saloon."

"You don't look as if you were damaged in any way," Samantha said. She stepped close to him, then circled him. "Your clothes aren't even dirty. If you were in a brawl, it had to be one of the shortest and neatest on record."

"Sam, honey, would you mind leaving us alone? I want to talk to John for a few minutes."

She pouted for a moment, then said, "Sure. You know where to find me." She started up the steps, then turned and said pointedly, "Both of you."

McCrae waited until she disappeared into the house before observing, "That gal fancies you a little, John. Be careful." He laughed, leaving Slocum to wonder whether he was being warned about Samantha McCrae or her father.

"Let's walk a little," McCrae said. "I don't want anybody to overhear what I got to say."

He took Slocum by the shoulder and directed him back toward the lane. Not until they were down among the trees did he continue. "I done some checking on Meyer, and I got a little more information, John. I don't mind telling you, I don't like what I hear, either. He was working down in Colorado about two years ago. Circumstances were pretty much like they are here. Cattlemen gettin' fenced in by them sheepherders. There was some trouble and they brought Meyer in. Three men got killed and a bunch more hurt. They never said Meyer done it, but from what I hear they know he did, they just couldn't prove it. He's ornery as a diamondback, only he don't give you no warning before he strikes."

"I saw a little bit of that this morning, Mr. McCrae. But I still don't see any reason I shouldn't move on."

"You don't have a reason, John. I know that. Except that I'm askin' you not to. Ben's a good man, but I don't know whether he's gonna do what I tell him on this thing. He don't like sheepherders. And some of the other boys, they're likely to use their guns instead of their brains. The way they see it, more sheep means less cows. That means less jobs for them. Meyer knows how to use that, and it wouldn't surprise me if he was already feelin' around, looking to see who he can use."

"You don't think Ben would throw in with him, do you?"

"I don't want to think that, but I just plain don't know, John."

Slocum was about to answer when he heard some riders approaching. The hoofbeats were rapid, as if the riders were in a big hurry. He looked down the lane, but the curving lines of trees prevented him from seeing more than fifty or sixty yards.

A moment later, several of the Double Deuce hands rounded the bend, Donaldson in the lead. He shouted something to the hands and reined in as the rest of them thundered on past. Slipping from the saddle, Donaldson let go of the reins and started toward his employer. He was grinning, but it wasn't a pleasant sight.

"So, there you are, Slocum," he said. "I wanted to talk to Mr. McCrae about you, and I guess it's just as well you're here. Don't want to be talkin' behind your back. That ain't gentlemanly."

"What's wrong, Ben?" McCrae asked.

"We had a little unpleasantness in town this morning. Slocum was there for part of it, and I reckon he already told you about it."

"Some, yeah, he did."

"Well, after he cut out on us," and he glared at Slocum to make his point, "Meyer got into another argument, this time with Kenny Randall."

"And . . ."

"Kenny's dead. Meyer shot him. It was a fair fight, and I got no complaint about that. But it seems to me like Meyer's on the wrong side. And I think that's Slocum's fault. He hadn't stirred the man up, Kenny wouldn't have been arguing with Meyer. It's that simple."

"Ben, I didn't stir him up," Slocum said. "You saw what happened. He was going to kill Dalton. I wasn't about to sit there and let that happen."

Donaldson spat. The gob of slime just missed Slocum's boots. The foreman didn't apologize, making it quite clear that the near miss had been no accident. "Dalton's a sheepdipper, Dan. And Slocum took his part. Should have drunk up and left, he didn't want to watch. But he had to stick his nose in. That set Meyer off. What happened next could have happened to anybody, but it was Kenny got in the way."

"Why blame me, Ben?" Slocum snapped. "Why not blame Meyer?"

"Meyer's scum, I know that. But he's on our side. We ought to just stay the hell out of his way and let him do his job. The sooner he does, the sooner he leaves."

"So it's all right with you, is it, if somebody gets killed? As long he smells like sheep instead of cows?"

"You can put it that way if you want, but that ain't what I mean. What I mean is them sheepdippers are buttin' in where they ain't wanted." He turned to McCrae then. "Dan, you want them out of here as bad as anybody, ain't that right?"

"Yeah, I do, Ben. I truly do. But I don't want to do it Meyer's way."

"Well, it's gonna be Meyer's way or it ain't gonna happen. I was talkin' to Frank Ramsey, from the Broken A, and he tells me some of the Broken A boys want to start a shootin' war right now."

"I won't have it, Ben. I just won't."

"We're gonna lose hands, Dan. I can tell you that right now. Duncan's already quit. Gone to work for Ramsey. I don't think he'll be the last one, neither."

"I'm sorry to hear that. Duncan's a good man. A bit of a hothead when he gets some whiskey under his belt, but he never let that stop him from giving me a good day's work. But I don't see what that has to do with John."

"I'll tell you what it has to do with Slocum, Dan. The boys don't like that he stuck up for Dalton. It's that simple. It's like he took sides, and he took the wrong one, as far as they're concerned."

"Calm down, Ben. It sounds to me like he did the right thing. It sounds like it's something you would've done. Fact is, I'm surprised he had to do it, just up off a sickbed like he is."

Donaldson took a deep breath. "I know what you're sayin', Dan. But . . ." He shook his head then, uncertain what to say. "I don't know what to think. You're right about Dalton. I don't have to like him to know he don't deserve killin'. Not like that, anyhow. He was pretty obnoxious, but . . ."

"Look, you tell the boys, anybody wants to quit, he can come see me. I won't stop 'im. I don't want anybody here who doesn't want to be here, and I sure don't want anybody riding for the Double Deuce if he's not gonna do what I say. I will fire anybody, including you, Ben, if I find out he's killin' sheep or, worse yet, takin' a shot at some sheepherder. I want them out of here, but not in a pine box. You clear on that, Ben?"

Donaldson nodded. "They won't like it."

"I don't give a damn whether they like it or not. I am not interested in mob justice, and that's just what this is. If we can't convince the sheep men to leave and we can't get the court to make them leave, then we got to learn to live with 'em. It's that Goddamned simple."

Donaldson nodded again, and walked to his horse. Holding the reins in his hand, he stuck one foot in a stirrup, then balanced there on one foot. "I'll do what I can, Dan. But I don't think I can keep 'em all happy."

He swung into the saddle, touched the brim of his hat and wheeled the horse around, kicked it with both spurs, and galloped off toward the bunkhouse.

"He's a good man," McCrae said. "And he's in a difficult position."

"He's a hothead, too, Mr. McCrae."

"He's got cause, John. But you see what I'm up against here. Please, wait a week before you make up your mind. After that, if you still want to go, I'll give you two months pay. No more arguments, just cash money. Fair enough?"

Slocum wasn't sure, but he nodded all the same. "Fair enough," he said. "I guess."

11

Slocum mounted the steps and entered the house. Samantha was nowhere to be seen, and he continued down the carpeted hallway to the stairs. On the landing, he stopped and looked around at the house. It gave every evidence of Dan McCrae's success. Thick oriental carpets covered the polished floors, leaving gleaming borders of oiled wood showing on their edges. The furniture, too, shone in the sunlight flooding through two pairs of ceiling-to-floor windows on the back wall.

He could just see into McCrae's study, where a gun rack mounted behind a large walnut desk held three English shotguns, their shining barrels elaborately engraved from their muzzles all the way to their trigger guards. In the drawing room, which was flooded with light pouring in through French doors, a piano, its wood as dark as coal, sat in one corner. A vase full of cut flowers was the only touch of color. A hand-tinted photographic portrait of the late Mrs. McCrae stood next to the vase. Another, of Samantha standing beside a pony, stood beside it.

McCrae had every reason to want to protect his way of life. He had done very well for himself, and Slocum had no doubt McCrae had worked hard to accumulate his possessions. That kind of wealth, though, brought with it the temptation to see the rest of the world as if from a very great distance. What was yours was important. What wasn't didn't really matter all that much except when it might cost you some of what you already had.

Slocum went back down the stairs and entered the drawing room. He stood in front of the piano, then picked up the portrait of Mrs. McCrae in its silver frame. She had been a handsome woman, and it wasn't hard to see where Samantha got her looks. And the mother's determined set of jaw had not skipped a generation, either.

Slocum set the portrait back on the piano, leaned over to sniff the flowers, then picked up Samantha's portrait. He studied it closely, as if he were looking for something the camera might have revealed that was not visible in the woman herself. But there was nothing. Setting the portrait back on the piano, he turned to see Dan McCrae watching him.

"Emma's been dead two years," he said, his voice noticeably husky. "And I still can't believe it."

"She was a beautiful woman."

"She was a tough woman, John. In many ways much tougher than I could ever be. Sam has some of that in her, too. It was for them that I built this place. I wanted Emma to have the best money could buy. She went to Europe once, just after the house was finished, and came back with a sack full of receipts. Stuff was showing up here at all hours of the day and night for months after she came home. A piano, dishes, crystalware, rugs, you name it. And I didn't give a damn about the money. Emma wanted it and I could pay for it, so what difference did it make? But I'd give every damn penny I have, if only . . ." He shrugged and turned away.

"Then, when Sam was old enough for school, Emma made sure she went to the best one back east. For Emma, it was the best or nothing. Only the best would do. Sam's like that, too. I guess she's her mother's daughter." McCrae turned back and brushed away the shining track of a tear with an idle swipe of his right hand. "That's why it's so important to me that this business not get out of control, John. You have no idea what it would mean if I had to lose all this, and leave nothing behind for Sam."

McCrae swept a hand around the drawing room. "This isn't just a house to me. It's a monument, in a way. A memorial to that woman." He pointed toward the portrait. "Now, Sam's all I have left of her. Sam, and all these damned *things*." He shook his head. "But things just aren't enough. If anything were to happen to this place, I don't know what I'd do."

"Nothing's going to happen, Mr. McCrae."

"Have you ever seen a range war, John? I mean a real one? Nobody's safe. Not men, not women, not even children. Animals get killed, fields get burned, and houses get destroyed. Damn it, whole lives get destroyed, John. I won't have that happen here. Not at any cost."

"I understand. I'll do what I can, but . . ."

"Oh, I know you can't promise anything more than that you'll try. You're the only one I can trust, John, because you're the only one who doesn't have a vested interest in the outcome. You've been drifting for a long time. I know that. And I know it's none of my damned business why, which is why I haven't asked you anything about your past. No matter what happens here, you can stay clear of it, stand back and see what makes sense. That's something money can't buy. And it's something I need. You have to help me, John. Please?"

"I said I'd stay, Mr. McCrae. That's all I can do."

McCrae nodded slowly. He sat on the piano bench, poised his fingers over the keys, and lowered them slowly. A full-throated chord filled the room. Then, ever so slowly, McCrae bent over the keyboard, his fingers suddenly no longer the thick, calloused instruments of a working man, but the delicate instruments of a musician.

Chord after chord swelled and died, then McCrae began to play a melody, which Slocum remembered from the War Between the States. It was an Irish air, the name of which he didn't know, but which the Yankee pickets used to play on harmonicas during the long nights when they were just a musket's shot away, as lonely in the darkness as their rebel counterparts.

McCrae slammed one final chord, then closed the keyboard cover. "Beautiful song, isn't it? It's the only thing I can play. My mother used to sing it to me when I was a child. It was the only thing that kept me sane in the steerage of that damn ship when we came over. Emma taught me to play it. She said I had a good ear, but I think she was just trying to make me feel good."

Not knowing what else to say, Slocum nodded. "It sounded fine," he said, then changed the subject. "I think I'd better move back to the bunkhouse. The hands already resent me if what Ben said is true. If I stay here, that'll only get worse. And I think I better go back out to Bracken's Creek. I'm well enough that I can help run the fence."

"Whatever you want, John. Do what you think best."

Slocum backed out of the drawing room, then started up the stairs for the second time. As he reached the second floor, the strains of "Londonderry Air" drifted up the stairwell after him. He went in to his room, then walked to the bed and sat down.

He took off his gunbelt and draped it over the back of a chair alongside the bed. Lying back, he closed his eyes, and a wave of exhaustion swept over him. His shoulder had held up well, but there was a dull ache, and he felt as if all his energy had been leached away by the morning.

He fell asleep without intending to. And, as it had every night since he'd been shot, the morning in Rock Falls Canyon came back to him as real as if it were actually happening. Once more he could feel the cold water in the creek as he waded in, and hear the roar of the waterfall behind him as he lay down on the creek bank to slake his thirst.

And he could hear the gunshots. He jerked, and came half awake with the first shot, then settled back down into the dream. He could see the sun above him now, and feel the water as it closed over him after he'd been hit. For some reason, he didn't feel the wound itself, and he wasn't sure he heard the shot that had hit him. Then he was rushing along on the current, one arm limp at his side, the other scrabbling for handholds on the stony bottom to haul himself along.

The entrance loomed up in front of him, and he felt the ground move as he tried to get to his feet. He managed to stand, but still the ground moved, and then he realized it wasn't the ground at all that was moving, but the mattress on which he lay.

Opening his eyes, he saw Samantha McCrae sitting on the end of the bed.

"You were having a bad dream," she said. Then, as if not sure, she added, "Weren't you?"

He nodded. "Yeah, I was."

"How's the arm?"

"All right."

"Are you sure?"

"I'm sure, Miss McCrae."

"Good." She crawled along the edge of the mattress then, and lay beside him. He moved over to make room for her. Turning to look him in the eye, she asked, "Good enough to hold me?"

"Yes, but I don't think it's a good idea."

"No, I don't suppose you would. I might even agree with you. But I don't care."

"What about your father?"

"You don't have to hold him, even if he asks." She smiled at him, then stuck out her tongue with an impish grimace. "I love saying stupid things like that. It makes me forget how much I hate being grown-up."

"Do you, really?"

She shook her head, then curled against him. "Yes, I do." She draped an arm across his chest, and he lay flat, very near the edge of the bed. Her face was hidden by the cascade of dark hair now, and her words were muffled as she buried her face in his chest. He could feel her fingers slipping inside his shirt, then playing with the hair on his chest.

"Is anything wrong?" he asked.

She nodded.

"Do you want to talk about it?"

"Actually," she said, "I want to do anything *but* talk about it. I wish I could forget all about it, but I can't. Just be still and hold me."

He flattened his right hand across her back, patted her gently, then stroked her shoulders. Even motionless, her body betrayed the strength in her, the taut muscles of her back and shoulders prominent under his fingertips.

Withdrawn from his shirt, her hand slid across his stomach and under his belt. He could feel the heat of her palm, then her fingers playing with the curls of hair at their tips. He felt himself stirring and shifted his hips uncomfortably. But Samantha didn't seem to notice.

She kissed him, her lips nestling in the curve above his collarbone. "John," she whispered.

"What?"

"You're not really going to leave, are you? I mean, not for a while?"

"Not for a while, no."

"Good." Her hand slid further down, and her fingers curled around his erection.

"I don't think that's a good idea," he said.

She squeezed gently, then stroked him slowly. "Why not?"

"Because I—"

"Just be still," she whispered. Her fingers slid along the length of him, then back, and once more "I think . . . oh, never mind." She lay there slowly stroking him, hampered by his clothing, but making no move to unbutton the fly of his jeans. As her hand moved faster and faster, he felt himself pressing against the stiff cloth. Samantha was breathing faster now, her breath hot on his throat.

Then, just when he thought he couldn't stand it much longer, his cock jerked spasmodically and he felt the release. Samantha moistened her fingers with the ejaculation then curled them around him once more. After stroking him a few more times, she sat up abruptly, unbuckled her belt and guided his hand into the dampness between her legs. "It's your turn," she whispered.

12

Slocum was given the cold shoulder in the bunkhouse. Most of the hands ignored him completely, and those few who bothered to acknowledge his presence tossed thinly veiled insults in his direction. He lay down to sleep on his bunk, wondering how twenty-four hours could have brought about so complete a change in his life.

It didn't seem logical that so simple a thing as stepping in to protect an innocent man could have invited such contempt, but it had, and there was little he could do about it. He hoped that a night's sleep would make all of them see things with a little more clarity, and maybe just a little more charity, the following day. But whether it did or not, he was going to have to work with these men for at least a week. He had promised Dan McCrae, and a promise was not something he gave lightly or disregarded easily once he had given it.

He fell asleep with difficulty, images of Samantha McCrae shouldering aside vivid pictures of the morning's confrontation with Cord Meyer. The next few days would be interesting, if nothing else. He didn't think he had to worry about the men turning on him, but he was determined to watch his back, just to be sure. And it now seemed that his task would be even more difficult. Not only were the men not likely to let anything slip, it was unlikely they would say anything at all as long as he was in earshot.

But he hadn't promised McCrae to do anything but listen and keep his eyes open. If he heard nothing, it wouldn't be his fault.

Sleep finally came, as he knew it would, and the sky wasn't even gray yet. He slept deeply, the strain of the previous day having taken him all the way to the bottom of the well. And when Cookie Mercer banged on his triangle to wake them, Slocum bolted upright like a man shot out of a cannon. He realized that his nerves were still frayed, and that the little sleep he managed to get had done little to reassure him, or to restore him, no matter what he wanted to believe.

Breakfast was quick and dirty. Beans and strips of steak were both seared nearly beyond recognition with Cookie's typical lack of attention. But Slocum was hungry, and chewed without tasting anything. By six thirty, the men were in the saddle, and three more wagonloads of fence posts lumbered over the hill behind McCrae's lavish home. Once Slocum crossed the ridge, he knew he would be on his own.

But at this point, angry as he was at the other hands, he almost welcomed the solitude. If they wanted to make an issue of his actions, he was more than ready for them. It might do him good to get it all out into the open, maybe even throw a punch or two.

There wasn't much chance he could win a fistfight, not with his arm still so vulnerable. But he had the almost uncontrollable urge to smash something, to drive his fist as hard as he could, and as often, into something unyielding, something that would soak up the anger and keep on soaking it until he was drained.

By the time they reached Bracken's Creek, he had

calmed down. Like the others, he groaned as he saw the wagons full of coiled wire. And like them, he swung out of the saddle almost eagerly. The desire to avoid the work could not be realized, so the best way to get it over with was to work as hard as possible for as long as possible.

He worked with Ben Donaldson for the first two hours, alternately holding posts until the dirt was filled in around them, or shoveling the loose soil into cones around the post in Donaldson's big hands, then tamping the dirt down until the post was secure.

Running the wire behind him and Donaldson, another pair of hands hammered staples into the roughly hewn pine. The echo of the hammer blows was incessant, slapping back at all of the men from distant hillsides, only partly muffled by the tall grass. On the slight breeze, the sound of milling cattle drifted toward them, as if to remind them why they were bothering to work so hard.

As far as Slocum knew, none of the other cattlemen were fencing their lands. Like most ranchers, they took the position that grazing land was open to everyone. It was the small owners who were in love with wire and wooden posts. As long as you didn't own too much land, it was easy enough to fence it in. It showed the world that somebody inside the wire was determined to defend what was his, and that a man who ignored that fence was reckless at best, and at worst taking his life into his own hands.

But Dan McCrae was not the run-of-the-mill cattleman. He had taken the trouble to file extensive claims on his property, and he was determined to keep sheep off the grazing land, even if it meant enough wire to stretch all the way to Cheyenne and back. He could afford it, and he had nothing else to spend the money on, so why not? What difference did it make, really, if the open range was ripped to pieces by politicians?

The problem was, of course, that a big herd needed a lot more grass than McCrae could fence in. According to Ben Donaldson, the only man who had spoken more than two words to Slocum all morning, McCrae's plan was to run his cattle on the open range as long as possible, saving the grass inside the fence from the sheep, and making sure there was plenty of it.

He had tried to talk all the ranchers into doing the same, but their position was that bullets were cheaper than wire, and they didn't require maintenance. The attitude was a carryover from a simpler time, but most of the ranchers preferred that time, because it meant they could do what they pleased and back up what they'd done with a Winchester and a Colt instead of a sheaf of papers some lawyer tried his damnedest to make unintelligible.

There was something to be said for that attitude, Slocum thought. But it was shortsighted, and he knew it. Wyoming, like most of the other territories, was doing its best to encourage settlement. That meant land had to be made available, and a man could do what he wanted with whatever was his. The days of the open range were numbered, and Dan McCrae seemed to be the only rancher within five hundred miles to understand that simple fact.

The sheepherders were in the same boat, but their flocks were smaller, and the animals didn't need as much grass as the steers. The meatpackers in Chicago and St. Louis and Kansas paid by the pound. The more your steers ate, the more money they brought in. It didn't take a degree in mathematics to see that more sheep meant less grass, and less grass meant lower prices for everybody.

Grunting as he drove the next post into the ground with a heavy hammer, Donaldson said, "I reckon me and you ought to have a little talk, John."

"You're the boss, Ben."

"No, I'm not. Dan McCrae is the boss. Because if he wasn't, you wouldn't be here now. I'd have fired your butt. But that don't mean I don't respect what you done. I do, believe me. And I even think maybe you done the right thing, John. But I been here for nine years.

I got a stake in this place. So do most of the other boys."

"And I don't, is that what you mean?" Slocum leaned on the shovel, watching the foreman's tanned face as he tried to find the right words.

"Yeah, that's what I mean. If this mess blows up, it'll take a lot of us with it. You can just climb on your horse and ride the hell out of Wyoming, go wherever the hell you want. I can't do that. I'm too old, too close to being broke down. I can't start over, so I got to hang on to what I got."

"And you think it's all right for a man like Cord Meyer to beat a drunken man into a bloody pulp?"

"Depends on who that drunken man is. If it's Ray Dalton, I don't much care one way or the other, to tell you the truth. If Dalton gets hisself killed, I don't think I'd even mind that too much. I know Meyer's a bad egg. But at least he's our egg. That makes all the difference, if you see what I mean."

"I see what you mean, Ben. I just don't agree with you, that's all."

"I respect that. And I respect the fact that you say so up front. A man don't have the guts to say what he thinks, then he ain't much of a man, in my book. I got to give you credit. But I got to warn you to be careful, too. There's some of the boys wouldn't mind if yours were the next nose Meyer broke. And they'd rather it was your neck that got broke."

Donaldson dropped the hammer then draped his folded hands over the top of the post. "Watch your back, John. I guess that's all I really mean to tell you. I won't stand by and watch somebody backshoot you. But if Meyer, or anybody else, for that matter, goes head-to-head with you, I'll be sittin' on my hands, most likely."

"Fair enough, Ben. To tell you the truth, I pretty much figured I was on my own. And I don't blame you. You do what you have to do. But I have to tell you that I'm only staying on here for two reasons—first, because

Mr. McCrae asked me to. He's afraid Meyer will get somebody killed. He doesn't want that to happen, and neither do I. The truth is—and this is the other reason—I suspect Meyer might have had something to do with the dead beeves, and with whoever tried to kill me. I don't think he did it himself, because I don't think he would have missed. But I aim to find out. And if I have to go through you to get to Meyer, I'll do it."

Donaldson straightened, clapped his hands to rid them of dirt and splinters, and said, "Well, then, I guess we each of us know where the other one stands."

Slocum nodded.

"One more thing," Donaldson said, bending to retrieve the hammer. "You watch out for Duncan."

"I'm not worried about him."

"No, it ain't what you think. He's kind of sweet on Sam. She hasn't paid him no attention, never did, and most likely never will, but it ain't no secret she's been givin' you the eye. Probably it ain't nothing, but if he starts blamin' you for takin' Sam away from him, he just might do something stupid. He's a good boy, and I don't want him to get himself hurt."

"There's nothing between Miss McCrae and me."

"I don't know if there is or if there isn't, and I don't much care. She's an awful good-looking gal, but it ain't my business who she likes and who she don't like. What I'm sayin' is that if Davey *thinks* there's somethin' between you and Sam . . . well, you know what I mean . . ."

Slocum shook his head. "I don't think I—"

The gunshot interrupted him. Donaldson looked at him. "What the hell was that?"

"Rifle shot," Slocum answered.

Donaldson turned to look back toward the creek, where some of the hands were taking a break, but everything looked normal. One of them was standing, hands on hips, looking up toward Slocum and the foreman. Cupping his hands to make a megaphone, he shouted, "Ben, you hear that?"

Donaldson started to run toward the trees. "Sure did, Reilly," he called.

Slocum sprinted after him, catching the foreman and then passing him on the downward slope. "Everybody here?" Slocum asked.

"What's it to you?" Reilly Cohan snapped. "Mind your own—"

"No," another hand said. "Pete Renske and Rick Brown went up the creek aways." The hand looked around, counting heads, then announced, "they ain't back yet."

By this time, Donaldson had joined them. "Then you spread out and find 'em, and make it quick!"

13

Another rifle shot boomed across the valley, and Slocum knew it was no ordinary rifle. It was deep, a resonant clap of thunder that had to be a buffalo gun. There was no sign of the two missing hands and no indication of the shooter's location.

"Pete," Donaldson hollered. "Rick? You all right?" But there was no answer. "Where'd you say they went, Bobby?" Donaldson asked.

Bobby Pietras shrugged. "Said they was gonna take a walk, get their minds off work. That's all I know."

Slocum moved down along the creek bank, waded across to the other side, and into the brush. Behind him, he could hear Donaldson calling to both men once more, and once more getting no answer.

Creeping through the brush, he reached a point where it thinned a little, and let him look up the hillside toward the opposite ridge. He didn't see anything out of the ordinary. There was no sign of either man or horse anywhere on that side of the creek.

There had been no answering fire, and he thought that

it might just have been a hunter, maybe taking a shot at a pronghorn. It certainly wasn't a gunfight.

Straining to hear the faintest sound, he heard only birds in the trees behind him, and the whisper of a faint breeze through the leaves. The grass on the hillside rippled, sending waves of light shimmering and racing from one end of the valley to the other.

Shaking his head, he backed into the brush again, turned and recrossed the creek. Donaldson was standing with the other cowhands. The men seemed baffled, and more than a little worried.

As Slocum approached Reilly Cohan glared at him. "You better hope that wasn't your friend Dalton takin' a shot at Pete and Ricky, Slocum."

"Ray Dalton is no friend of mine."

"You'd never know it, by the way you stuck your neck out for him yesterday."

"You saw what happened to him, Reilly, what he looked like when Meyer was done kicking his face in. Was I supposed to stand there and watch? Or should I have cheered him on?"

"He wasn't done, you stopped him. I figure Meyer had three, four more good whacks in him yet. But you had to stick your nose in."

"Slocum's right, Reilly. Dalton was a mess. No way on God's green earth he's out roamin' around with a long gun after a beating like that. He's lucky if his eyes ain't swole shut for a month." Donaldson was losing his temper, and Slocum didn't know whether it was at Reilly Cohan's insensitivity or because the two hands were missing.

"That's not the point, Ben," Reilly said. "I—"

"That's enough, Reilly. The point is, Pete and Rick ain't here, and they don't answer when we call. Now, I don't like to make up trouble because there's enough of it around already. But we heard two shots, and we got two men missing. I don't like that sort of arithmetic. I want you boys to get your asses up in the saddle and find them two. And I want you to do it now, with no damn arguments and no bickerin', you understand? Slocum's gonna be working here for a while, so you might as well get used to it."

Cohan grumbled, but he knew Donaldson was right. It was more important to find the missing men than to snipe at Slocum, so he shrugged and moved off to the makeshift remuda, where the horses were tethered to a lariat run between two cottonwoods.

Donaldson looked at Slocum. "You got any ideas?" he asked.

"None. But like you, I don't like the way it looks. Not too likely they fell asleep. And if they did, the gunshots probably would have awakened them. I think we better find them, and quick."

"All right. Take two of the men with you, and ride up to the top of the ridge. Sounded to me like them gunshots came from somewheres up there. Maybe you can find something. Besides, it'll give you a good look down into the valley. And you tell the boys you bring along that if they give you any lip, I will personally rip their lungs out."

Slocum smiled. "Nothing like being the messenger who brings bad news." He smiled again, and Donaldson glared at him for a moment, then broke into a grin.

"You're all right, Slocum. You got balls. I got to give you that, for sure. And if I was a bettin' man, which I am thankful I ain't, I'd bet we find them bent over an empty bottle of cheap whiskey."

"I hope you're right, Ben." Slocum grunted his thanks for the compliment and moved toward his horse. He told Bobby Pietras and Jack O'Lone to come with him. Pietras shook his head, looked at Donaldson, then mounted up. O'Lone was more belligerent. "The hell I'm gonna ride with you, Slocum," he said.

"You want to draw pay on the Double Deuce, you'll git on that horse and do like Slocum tells you," Donaldson barked. O'Lone opened his mouth to argue, but Donaldson waved his hand angrily. "I don't want to hear it, Jocko. You do like I say, now."

As Slocum swung into the saddle, he heard two more gunshots, this time from a pistol. He kicked the chestnut hard and raced along the bank, hollering for the two hands to follow him. He wasn't crazy about riding into a gun battle with two allies who were, at best, reluctant, but there was no time to do anything else.

Another shot from the long gun boomed across the hillside, and this time, Slocum spotted a patch of smoke that had to be from the rifle. Up at the north end of the valley, it drifted just above the crest of the hill, a thin veil of blue-gray that broke into tatters as he raced toward it. There was still no sign of the gunman, and no sign of the missing hands.

Slocum knew he was riding right up under the gunman's muzzle now, risking a bullet, but it was the only way to catch him. As he charged parallel to the creek, he tried to stay low in the saddle, and close to the brush cluttered alongside the streambed.

He could see a bit of the ridge across the valley, but not much. Easing away from the valley bottom a bit, he pushed the chestnut harder, giving the horse its head and trying to watch the ridgeline for a silhouette that might give away the gunman's location.

There was another shot from a handgun, and this time he got a fix on its location. The rifle boomed once more, and Slocum realized it was definitely a buffalo gun. It sure as hell was bigger than a Winchester carbine, he thought.

Suddenly, there was a flurry of motion in the grass, near where the pistol shot had originated. Then someone straightened up. A man on his knees raised a pistol and pointed it toward the ridge, but his back exploded in a spray of gore that was still fanning out across the grass when the sound of the buffalo gun thundered down through the valley.

Slocum cursed under his breath, turned to see where Pietras and O'Lone were, then used the reins to lash the chestnut twice. He saw someone stand high atop the ridge, just the head and shoulders of a man who quickly disappeared.

The range was long, maybe seven hundred yards. It was a hell of a shot, Slocum thought, shaking his head in admiration at the marksmanship. He thought of the explosion of blood he'd just seen, and knew the man was dead, but it didn't change the fact that the gunman had to be remarkable.

Turning to Pietras and O'Lone, he jerked a thumb toward the spot where he'd seen the figure, and slowed the chestnut just enough to let the two hands catch up. "On the ridge," he shouted. "Just caught a glimpse of him. Let's go!"

Slocum changed direction, headed toward the trees and nudged the chestnut on into the brush, slowing even more to let the horse pick its way to the creek bank. He pushed on across, through the trees and out into the grass on the far side, then dug his spurs in. The chestnut spurted forward, shaking its head as Slocum urged it to a full gallop.

The two cowboys were right behind him. As they charged past the spot where he'd seen Rick Brown get hit, he pointed, and turned to see O'Lone peel off and dismount. The chestnut was giving it everything it had, barely slowing as horse and rider started uphill. Slocum kept his eyes trained on the ridge, sweeping them from side to side, hoping that if the gunman were still there, he'd have warning, enough time to hurl himself from the saddle.

But there had been nothing to see, not even a hint of color gliding through the grass, the brim of a hat, the glint of sunlight on a rifle barrel. Nothing.

At the top of the hill, he headed parallel to the ridge. Unlike the last time he'd pursued the echo of gunshots over the hill, this time there was no rider anywhere in evidence. There was a trail through the grass, and that was all. A hundred yards from where he'd reached the crest, he saw a depression in the grass, and dismounted.

It was obvious that the gunman had lain there for a long time. The grass was pressed flat in a large oval, almost seven feet on its long axis, as if the sniper had changed position several times, probably tracking his target, waiting for the right moment. He could have been there all morning, Slocum thought, watching us. And waiting.

Pietras sat on his horse, which kept jerking its head, fighting the bit as the rider tried to keep him still. "See anything?" he asked.

Slocum shook his head. "No, I . . . wait a minute. What's this?"

Something had caught his eye in the grass just outside the oval depression. He reached down, parted the grass and picked up a cartridge casing. He looked at it closely and recognized it as a Sharps .50 caliber, the favorite of buffalo hunters. The Sharps was deadly at nearly a thousand yards, according to those who favored it. One slug was capable of knocking down a bull buffalo in full charge, and at half a mile, some said. He didn't want to think what it had done to Rick Brown.

Combing the grass with his fingers, he found three more shells, all for the Sharps. It was a single-shot rifle, which meant a man willing to use it had to be awfully confident of his ability or have nerves of steel—and probably both. A man like Cord Meyer, for instance, he thought.

But he hadn't seen the gunman clearly enough to identify him. And he didn't know whether Meyer favored a Sharps, or even if he had one. But he meant to find out.

"Ain't you gonna follow him, Slocum?" Pietras asked.

Slocum shook his head. "No sir, Bobby, I ain't. He's probably long gone, and if he isn't, I won't give him the satisfaction of making a good target for him."

"But he'll get away."

"If it's who I think it is, he won't be going anywhere for a while. We'd best get on back to the others. Somebody's got to ride into Bracken and tell Sheriff Hansen."

Pietras nodded. "I guess you're right. Who do you think it is?"

"Hell, it's Meyer. Has to be."

"Naw. Meyer's on our side. I think it was one of them sheepherders. They got reason."

"They got reason, maybe. But I'd bet you everything I own, there isn't one of them could hit the side of a barn at fifty feet with a Sharps. And that shot was a good six hundred and fifty yards, probably more. You think Ray Dalton could pull that off? Cause if you do, Bobby, you might as well pack your kit and head on to Montana, because Wyoming is sheep country, as of right now."

Slocum tucked the shells into his shirt pocket, climbed back into the saddle, and started back down toward the creek. He could see Ben Donaldson, Jack O'Lone and three other men clustered around the spot where he'd seen Ricky Brown get hit. Donaldson looked up as he approached, watched him all the way down the hill, but said nothing until he dismounted.

Pietras slid from his saddle and trailed behind Slocum, then joined O'Lone and the others. "I never seen anything like it, Slocum," Donaldson said. "Blew a hole in them you could stick your fist in. Christ almighty, what the hell did he use?"

Slocum reached into his pocket, pulled one of the shell casings out and tossed it to Donaldson. The foreman whistled. "No wonder," he said.

"You said them . . ."

Donaldson nodded. "Yeah, he killed them both, by God. Pete and Ricky both. I hope to God I get my hands on him."

"First we got to find out who did it, Ben."

"Then we better do it quick, because the boys aren't gonna want to wait for too long. They smell sheep on somebody, they'll whip a rope around his stinkin' neck as quick as you please."

14

Slocum sat in the study, looking at the books, most of which were bound in leather and showed signs of heavy use. Dan McCrae finished scribbling his signature on a letter, then sat back. "All right, John," he said. "What's on your mind?"

"Cord Meyer."

"What about him?"

"Tell me everything you know about him. Even if it doesn't seem important."

"You think he killed those two boys, don't you? Pete Renske and Rick Brown . . ."

"I know he did, Mr. McCrae. What I don't know is how to prove it."

"Well, I told you most of what I know. But I'll run through it all again, if you think it'll help. He fought in the Civil War, with Grant, mostly. He was a lieutenant with the Fourth Cavalry for a while after the war, mostly posted out west. He either quit under a cloud or got run out, nobody seems real sure about that, after some nasty business with the Cheyenne. Seems like he and his men attacked a village of peaceful Indians. There were a lot of casualties, mostly women and children. There wasn't no court martial, but you and I both know that don't mean much. The army don't like to admit when its people are out of control, so they just suck in their bellies and ask you to resign."

"You said there was some killing on his last job, if I remember correctly."

"His last three or four, actually. He gave us references, and I been in touch with the people who hired him. Some of them have answered and some haven't. Where I can, I'm writing to more than one person, because folks only pass on what they think is important. You hire a man to do a job and somebody gets killed, well, maybe you don't much care about it, so you don't mention it. Maybe that's why you hired him in the first place. Not in so many words, exactly, but that's what you want and he knows it, so . . . well, naturally, that ain't something you necessarily want to tell nobody. But anyhow, two places in Colorado and one in New Mexico, there was some killing. Nobody brought charges, but then that ain't all that unusual. The law seems to work for the folks who pay the lawmen, don't it?"

"He use a buffalo gun?"

"Don't really know. I only seen him three, four times. Didn't see a buffalo gun. Why?"

"Because whoever killed Renske and Brown used a Sharps. I thought maybe you might know."

"Now that you mention it, he did some time as a buffalo hunter, three or four years ago, after he got out of the Cavalry. Maybe he's got a Sharps. I just don't know."

"Where's he staying?"

"Supposed to be at Jake Barton's place, but what I hear is he spends a lot of time out on the range, sometimes four, five days at a time. Comes and goes, Jake says. And he don't ask Meyer about it, because he figures the man's got a job to do, and you got to stay out of his way and let him do it."

Slocum nodded. "All right. Anything else you can tell me, Mr. McCrae?"

"That's about the whole shootin' match, John. I wish I could help, but . . ."

"I'm going to need a few days, Mr. McCrae, if I'm going to be any use to you. Staying on the work crew doesn't let me learn anything. The men don't want to talk, even if they know something, and I'm not sure that they do, so . . ."

McCrae stroked his chin before answering. "All right. I asked you to stick your neck out, so I guess I got to let you do things your way. Seems kind of strange, payin' a man to regulate a regulator. But I guess that's how it's got to be. You need anything?"

Slocum shook his head. "Just the time, is all."

"How long you figure it'll take? I mean, Sheriff Hansen is already lookin' into the killings. He won't take too kindly to the idea of you nosin' around in his business."

"Then don't tell him."

"I won't, but you can't really keep a thing like that secret for too long. Even if I was to make somethin' up, folks would figure it out sooner or later."

"Then we'll just have to hope it's later. You know, Mr. McCrae—"

"Damn it, John, why can't you just call me Dan. Ever'body else does."

"All right . . . Dan. Like I was saying, my first inclination was to pack my gear and ride on out of here, but the more I think about it, the more determined I am to stick it out. I don't like the idea of a man like Meyer getting paid to cause trouble. And I like the idea of him getting away with murder a whole lot less."

"Now, you ain't sure of that, John. If you're gonna go off talkin' like that, you got to be damn sure you can back up what you say."

"Oh, I'll be sure all right, Dan. I'll be sure. And you're going to have to help me. Anything you hear, you let me know. I'll cheek in with you every couple of days."

McCrae stood up. "I got to go," he said. "There's a meeting of the Cattleman's Association this afternoon."

"Will Meyer be there?"

McCrae shrugged. "I don't know. He's supposed to be, but as near as I can tell, he does what he damn well pleases. It's almost like we're workin' for him, instead of the other way around. I'll let you know."

He opened a drawer in the desk, pulled out an envelope and handed it to Slocum. "You take this, John. You might need it."

"What is it?"

"Open it."

Slocum did as he was told, pulled the flap open, and saw the top edge of a sheaf of bills. "Looks like two, three hundred dollars, Dan. What's this for?"

"Like I said. You might need it."

Slocum tossed the envelope onto the desk without counting the bills. "I don't want it. I take that money, that makes me no better'n Meyer. I'm not made that way."

"Suit yourself, John," McCrae said, reaching for his hat, clapping it on his head and tugging it tight. "You change your mind, it'll be here." He touched the brim of the hat and started for the door. "I'll see you around, John."

Slocum stood there, trying to sort through the conflicting emotions swirling inside him. Not until he heard McCrae's horse break into a gallop did he start out of the study. He was almost to the front door when Samantha called to him.

"John, wait a minute, please?" He turned around to see her descending the stairs. "I need to talk to you," she said. "It's important."

"All right." He watched her descend the stairs in bare feet, stop on the bottom step, and reach out to him. "Come on upstairs. I don't want to talk here."

She didn't wait for him to answer. Following her up the steps, he wondered what was on her mind. She had looked almost distraught, but he didn't have a clue as to what could be troubling her.

At the top of the stairs, she led him down the hallway, stepped into her room, and stood aside until he followed her in, then closed the door.

"What is it, Miss McCrae? Anything wrong?"

"I'm not sure. I just . . . well, I was in town this morning, and I heard some men talking. They were sitting in front of the Red Sombrero Saloon, as I went by. I went into Ackerman's—that's the milliner's—and I could hear them whispering."

"What about?"

"About you. Something bad's going to happen, I just know it. They said you weren't going to last. That it wouldn't be long before you got what was coming to you."

Slocum smiled. "I wouldn't worry about it, Miss McCrae. It's just talk. Men get a couple of drinks in them, they start talking big. Every colt's a stallion then, every shiny rock's a gold nugget, usually the size of your fist. I'm sure there's nothing to worry about."

"They sounded like they knew something. And I . . ."

"They're supposed to sound like they knew something. That's part of it, Miss McCrae. You want the man you're talking to to think you know something he doesn't. You can exaggerate all you want, just as long as you make it sound convincing." Slocum was trying to downplay her fears, despite his own concerns. He realized he was doing exactly the same thing he was talking about. But it was like looking through the other end of the telescope. He was trying to make everything small, the smaller and less consequential the better.

Samantha seemed to realize it. At least she wasn't taking his dismissal at face value. "But this was different. They named names."

"What names?"

"Dave Duncan, for one. And that man Meyer. His name was mentioned."

"Well, I thank you for the warning, but I wouldn't lose any sleep over it, if I were you."

She stepped toward him then, her hands clasped in front of her, fingertips just grazing her chin. "I do worry."

He reached out to pat her shoulder to reassure her, and she pressed herself against him. He knew she was tall, but he hadn't realized until that moment just how tall she was. The top of her head was at eye level. He held her for a moment, and buried his face in her hair. It smelled like lilac. He could feel her breasts against his chest and, almost in spite of himself, let his hands wander down her back until he felt the curve of her ass against his palms. He slipped his hands into the rear pockets of her jeans and pressed her hips against him.

"You worry too much, Sam," he said.

She shook her head. "Maybe I can't help it."

She stepped back then, and started to unbutton her denim shirt. When it came open, he gasped involuntarily. Her breasts were magnificent, firm and full, the smooth curves broken only by erect nipples. He started to shake his head, but her hands were already fumbling at her belt. She loosened it, unbuttoned the jeans and pulled them down to her knees, then kicked them all the way off.

The starkness of the triangle of glossy black hair looked almost out of place against the white skin.

"Can you undress yourself, or do you need help?" she asked, flashing him a lewd smile.

He undid his shirt buttons instead of answering her. Impatient, she knelt in front of him, worked his belt loose, then tugged his pants down without undoing the fly. Tangled in his jeans, he tried to step out of them, but they were caught on his boots, and Samantha pushed him backward, where he landed on the soft carpet, breaking his fall with both hands. He winced when the shock hit his wounded arm, but she didn't give him a chance to complain. Jerking his underpants down around his knees she straddled him, a wicked gleam in her eye.

"Are you up for this?" she asked. Glancing at his stiff cock, she said, "Stupid question, I guess."

Lifting her hips she poised herself over him. Slocum reached to cup her breasts in his hands as she started to lower herself. The tight black curls of her bush tickled him as she rocked her hips back and forth, suspended over him.

"Anybody there? Sam? Slocum?"

"It's my father," she said. Then, without blinking an eye, she engulfed him, slid all the way down and leaned over to plant a peck on his cheek before sliding up and off him and getting to her feet. "I guess we'll have to wait," she said. Her grin was maddening as she said, "Get your pants on, cowboy, before he comes up here."

Walking to the door, her perfect ass rocking on well-oiled hips, she leaned into the hall and called, "Be right down, Daddy."

15

Slocum scrambled to his feet, nearly falling over in his haste, tugged his underpants and jeans back up, and struggled to get into his shirt. Samantha was already dressed by the time he started on his buttons. She walked out into the hallway and started down the stairs.

As Slocum buttoned the last button on his shirt, he heard Dan McCrae ask, "Is Slocum here?"

"Yes, Daddy, he's upstairs. Why?"

"The sheriff is here. Wants to talk to him. Would you ask him to come on down." If he was surprised that Slocum was still there, Samantha didn't notice it.

"What about?"

"I think it's best we leave that to Slocum and the sheriff, don't you? Go get him, would you?"

"All right. I'll be right back."

"Tell him to hurry," McCrae shouted as Samantha bounded back up the stairs in her bare feet.

Slocum was waiting just inside the doorway. Samantha looked at him, her eyes wide with fear. "Daddy said . . ."

"I heard," Slocum said.

"What's it about, do you think?"

Slocum shook his head. "I don't know, but I guess I better go on down and find out."

He stepped through the door, running a hand through his hair, trying to straighten it a little. As he reached the top of the steps, he could see McCrae in the downstairs hall. The sheriff was standing beside him, hat in hand. He seemed uncomfortable, shuffling his feet and slapping the hat against his thigh. He glanced up with a distracted frown as Slocum started down the steps.

McCrae gave him a funny look, then looked beyond him, higher on the stairway, and Slocum turned to see Samantha starting down after him.

"You remember Merrill Hansen, don't you, John?"

Slocum nodded. "Sure. How are you, Sheriff?" He extended a hand, but Hansen looked at it strangely, as if wondering what it was. Then, almost as an afterthought, he took the hand and gave it a cursory shake.

"What can I do for you, Sheriff?" Slocum asked.

"Like to ask you a few questions, if I might."

"Sure thing. You get a lead on that bushwhacker already?"

"Not exactly. Glad to see you're up and around, though. You looked like hell the day I came out here."

"Well, I've been hurt worse, but not lately." Slocum laughed, but the sheriff didn't join him. Noticing the man's apparent anxiety, Slocum asked, "Anything wrong?"

"You mind comin' outside for a few minutes? Got something I want to show you."

"What?"

"You'll see."

Slocum looked at McCrae, who shrugged to suggest he had no idea what was going on. "Run into Merrill on the way to the Cattleman's Association meeting," he said. "When he said he was lookin' for you, I figured

I'd ride along, and see what it was all about."

"No need for you to stay, Dan," Hansen said. "This'll just take a few minutes. You got that meeting, so why don't you go on?"

McCrae started to argue, but Hansen waved him off. "Go on, Dan. This don't really concern you, anyhow. My business is with Mr. Slocum."

"You sayin' I can't stay?"

Hansen shook his head. "I'd rather you didn't. 'Sides, it ain't that important. You got better things to tend to, unless what I been hearin' is off the mark."

"That'll be the day, Merrill," McCrae laughed. "All right, then, I guess I'll go on to the meeting. John, you let me know what this is all about, will you? Soon as you find out?" He walked back to his horse, undid the reins at the post and swung up into the saddle. He sat there for a moment, his eyes almost squinting as he tried to understand what was happening. Then, with a shake of the head, as if to say he didn't and wouldn't understand, no matter how long he sat there, he wheeled the horse around and spurred it into a trot.

Samantha sat on the bottom step, her knees scrunched up under her chin. She wiggled her toes in the dirt, her head cocked slightly to one side. She never took her eyes off Hansen. Her unwavering gaze seemed to make the sheriff even more uncomfortable.

Turning and walking to his horse, Hansen untied a parcel that was laced to the back of his saddle. It was a blanket, but it stuck out stiffly on both sides, telling Slocum there was something rigid inside.

Walking back to where Slocum stood at the bottom of the steps, he said, "I got something here I want you to take a look at, if you would." His finger fumbled with one of the two strings keeping the blanket rolled and, when he couldn't get the knot undone, he raised the package to pop the string with his teeth.

No one spoke, and the snap of the twine sounded louder than it was in the silence. Hansen popped the second string, started to unroll the blanket, then changed his mind. He lowered the blanket roll and let it hang at his side.

"Maybe I should ask you a few questions first. You mind?"

Slocum shook his head. "Why should I mind?"

"Just being polite, is all, Mr. Slocum. That don't hurt, you know. Anyhow, I was wondering if you'd mind tellin' me where you were this afternoon?"

"What time?"

"Around noon, maybe a little before, I guess. Does it matter?"

"If you want to know exactly, it does, yeah. I came back here from Bracken's Creek. Pete Renske and Rick Brown got shot, as you know, and . . ."

"Terrible thing about them boys. I was afraid it was going to come to something like this. What with that Meyer, and all. Too much soup on the kettle, it's bound to boil over. That's what the missus says, anyhow. I ain't sayin' Meyer done it, understand? Probably he didn't. Most likely, it was one of them sheepherders, but if Meyer wasn't here, it probably wouldn't come to this. Anyhow, I don't know who done it, but I aim to find out, just like I aim to find out who gunned you. Might even be the same man, for all I know."

"Like I was saying, Sheriff," Slocum continued, "I came back here. I wanted to talk to Mr. McCrae."

"You mind saying what about?"

"Yeah, I do. If he says it's all right, then I'll tell you. But it's confidential."

Hansen nodded skeptically. "All right. And you was here the whole time?"

"Yes sir, I was."

"Must have had a lot to talk about."

"I suppose you could say that."

"I can vouch for Mr. Slocum, Sheriff. He's been here since about eleven thirty."

"Why are you asking, Sheriff?" Slocum asked. He didn't like the direction the questions were taking, and he was starting to feel uneasy.

"I'll get to that, Mr. Slocum. Just keep your pants on." He smiled at Samantha then, as if to suggest he knew more than he was revealing about the recent history of the garments in question. "You ever been to Ray Dalton's place, Mr. Slocum?" he continued.

"Nope. Never have."

"You could find it if you had to, though, is that right? I mean, you know where it is, don't you?"

"I have a general idea. I know Mr. McCrae and he have had a few run-ins because Dalton's property runs up against the Double Deuce over past Bracken's Creek."

"You see Ray Dalton this morning, did you? Or maybe Timmy, his boy?"

"When? While I was at the creek?"

Hansen nodded.

"No."

"You seen the gunman, though, the man who killed Renske and Brown, didn't you?"

"Saw a hat and some shoulders. Not enough to identify the man, if that's what you mean."

"You think it was Ray Dalton?"

"No, not really. I don't think I have an opinion one way or another, really. But I don't think it was Dalton, no."

"You mind saying why not?"

"I doubt if Dalton is capable of a shot like that. Not after that beating. And from what I hear, he doesn't even have a buffalo gun."

"Why do you think it was a buffalo gun?"

"You saw the bodies, Sheriff. You ever see an ordinary carbine slug put a hole like that in a man? Besides, I found some Sharps .50 caliber shell casings on top of the ridge, where the shots were fired."

"I know that. Ben give me one of 'em. But you didn't see the man, that what you said?"

"Right. I didn't see him clearly. I'm pretty sure that the man I saw was the shooter, but I don't know who he was."

"You have an idea, though, don't you?"

"Nothing that would hold up in court. Nothing I can prove. So I'd rather not say."

Hansen thrust the rolled blanket at Slocum so abruptly, it slammed into his chest. "You mind opening that blanket, Mr. Slocum?"

Slocum shrugged. "I suppose not." He unrolled the blanket, and let it fall to the ground. Inside was his Winchester carbine.

"You ever see that gun before, Mr. Slocum?"

"It's mine."

"That's what I thought. You sure about that?"

"Yeah, I'm sure. Where'd you get it?"

Hansen didn't answer the question, instead rushing to ask another of his own. "And you lost that Winchester over in Rock Falls Canyon, that right?"

"That's right. Why?"

"You sure you lost it?"

"Sheriff," Samantha interrupted, getting to her feet, "What's this all about? Mr. Slocum said he lost the rifle. My father bought him a new one to replace it. I was with him. You can ask Mr. Grisson, at the General Store. That's where Daddy bought it."

"Oh, I know that, Miss McCrae. I already checked on that. What I want to know is when Mr. Slocum seen this particular rifle last." He looked hard at Slocum then, waiting for an answer.

"The last I saw it was in Rock Falls Canyon. Nine days ago."

"You sure about that?"

Slocum was losing his patience. "Damn right, I'm sure. Now, you want to tell me what the hell this is all about?"

"I'm gonna have to ask you to come along with me, Mr. Slocum."

"What the hell for?"

"Somebody killed Ray Dalton and his boy late this morning, around noon." He nodded at the Winchester in Slocum's hand, then reached out to take it from him. "That there's the gun what done it."

Slocum shook his head. "Jesus Christ, you don't think I . . ."

"It's not what I think, Mr. Slocum. It's what I been told. I got witnesses. Three of 'em. I got no choice but to bring you in. I'm charging you with the murder of Ray Dalton and his son, Timmy."

16

Merrill Hansen closed the cell door, turned the key in the lock, and said, "I wish I could say I'm sorry about this, Slocum, but I ain't. And even if I was, the way things are, I don't have a choice."

"You think I killed Dalton, Sheriff?"

"I don't know, and that's the plain truth, Slocum. I know it don't make much sense. It isn't often a man risks his neck to save a man one day, then turns around and shoots him dead the next. But you got to understand one thing. We're not just talkin' about a feud here, or a range war, whatever the hell you want to call it. Ray Dalton was a nasty drunk and he sure had a fistful of enemies around here, some of which he earned by hard work. But we're also talkin' about the murder of an eleven-year-old boy, and the way I see it, murder don't come any more cold-blooded than that."

"Sheriff, even if I had reason to shoot Dalton, which I didn't, I had no reason to shoot a child."

"Nobody did, Slocum, nobody at all, so that don't help convince me one way or the other. But I'll tell you this, whether it was you or whether it was somebody else, when I find the man, it wouldn't surprise me if I have to shoot him trying to escape. If you catch my drift . . ."

"That would be murder, too, Sheriff."

"Maybe. Or maybe it would just be justifiable homicide. One thing I know, and that's that there ain't no excuse for shootin' that boy. And I mean to see that the man who done it pays the price for it, whether he stretches a rope or goes to the cemetery four hundred grains heavier than he is right now. Either way's just fine by me."

"How can you be sure you have the right man, Sheriff? Suppose you make a mistake."

Hansen looked at him, but his only reply was a grunt.

"How long do I have to stay here?" Slocum asked.

"That depends on Judge Lassiter. He might set you bail, but I know Roy Lassiter a long time, and I wouldn't count on havin' that much money, if I was you."

Slocum watched the sheriff walk out of the cell block and close the heavy wooden door behind him. He could see Hansen's face through the grating as the sheriff locked the outer door. Then, with a jingle of heavy keys, Hansen was gone and Slocum was alone.

He felt like a fool. He had had his chance to ride on out, to leave the Double Deuce in his dust, but he hadn't done it. He had let Dan McCrae talk him into staying on, like he was some high-priced Pinkerton stock detective, and now he was an inch away from stretching a rope for a crime he didn't commit. He wished to Christ he had followed his instincts and left Bracken far behind him.

Hansen's anger was probably typical of the people around Bracken, and Slocum had no trouble understanding it. An eleven-year-old boy was not supposed to be the victim in this kind of situation. It was sweaty cowhands, and paunchy ranchers who were supposed to be shooting at sheepherders in suspenders and checkered shirts. But it hadn't worked out that way. McCrae had been right about one thing—Cord Meyer had not ridden into Bracken empty-handed; he had come with a passel of grief for the townspeople.

Looking around the cell, Slocum inventoried the meager furnishings. There was a cot with a striped mattress, probably filled with straw, and a single blanket that seemed about evenly divided between faded wool and moth-holes. In one corner of the eight by ten cell, a rusted bucket sat on its rim, useful as a stool or a place to deposit one. And that was it, except for his shadow.

He cursed softly, almost afraid to give full vent to the anger he could turn only on himself. He'd heard stories of men who hanged themselves with their own belts rather than spend a single night in jail, even for something so tame as drunk and disorderly conduct. He wasn't about to give in to that sort of insanity, but trapped in a room that size, a lot of men he'd known would feel so crowded they'd leave any way they could manage it, even to the point of choking the life out of themselves with a knotted strip of blanket or the sleeves of a shirt.

He kept telling himself that he had to think things through, try to find an explanation for his predicament that made some kind of sense. He knew there couldn't be witnesses to his alleged murder, because he hadn't killed anyone. And he hadn't been anywhere near the Dalton place, so it couldn't be a simple case of adding two and two to come up with five. That left only two possibilities—either the killer had looked like him in some way, which didn't strike him as all that likely, or he was deliberately being framed for a crime he hadn't committed, which, on the face of it, seemed to make even less sense.

But all he had to do was look around him, see the striped shadow on the floor cast by the bars on the windows, to know that someone was taking it seriously indeed. He couldn't blame Merrill Hansen for trying to do his job, but he had to find some way to get out of jail, because as long as Hansen thought he had the killer, he wouldn't be looking too hard for an alternative suspect.

He wished he had thought to ask Hansen who the witnesses were. The sheriff surely would tell him, because a man had a right to know the names of those who accused him, whatever the crime. Unless Hansen was in somebody's pocket. He didn't know the man all that well, but to Slocum it seemed improbable. More likely, he thought, Hansen had no reason not to accept the testimony from the supposed witnesses, which meant it couldn't have been Cord Meyer. Hansen didn't know Meyer at all, and from the sound of things, he didn't like him much, either. Which meant he wouldn't trust Meyer, so the witnesses had to be somebody else.

All sorts of explanations, each more fanciful than the last, began to suggest themselves to him. Maybe Dalton had been killed by one of the cattlemen. Maybe he had been killed by one of the sheepdippers who had a grudge and saw the chance to pin the crime on someone else. But why me, he wondered.

And there was still the attempt on Slocum himself. Since that had failed, maybe this was another way to get him out of circulation. But nobody had a reason to want that, except maybe Cord Meyer. But Meyer himself hadn't had that reason until after the first shooting. Or had he?

Slocum was finally forced to admit that he just didn't know enough, didn't have enough information, to construct any sort of plausible explanation. And he sure as hell wasn't going to get it sitting on his ass in this God damned cell. He had to get out, and he knew it had to be soon. With tensions rising in Bracken, there was even a chance that a lynch mob might decide to take the law into its own hands. And whatever else he knew, he was certain he hadn't been born to stretch a rope.

Slocum climbed up on the cot, felt the boards holding the mattress begin to bend under his weight, and grabbed hold of the window bars. He jerked them, but they were solid. If he was going to get out, it wouldn't be that way. He looked out at the afternoon light and could see the mountains far in the distance. As he watched, a faint black smear raced across the rolling hills out beyond the edge of town and it took him a moment to realize that it was the shadow of a cloud. Craning his neck, he tried to pick it out, but he just couldn't see enough of the sky.

He jerked the bars in frustration, harder than the first time, sending a stab of pain through his wounded arm. Ignoring the pain, he jerked the bars a third time, then threw himself back away from the window and dropped to the floor.

Lying down on the cot, he propped his head on folded hands, and stared at the ceiling. A crazy quilt pattern of cracks and scratches made it look like a diagram of a puzzle. With nothing else to do, he amused himself, trying to find familiar figures in the cracks the way he had looked for animals and people in the clouds sailing overhead all those years ago in Georgia.

But as if to remind him how little he understood his present predicament, the ceiling defied all his efforts. And after an hour, he closed his eyes, figuring he might as well try to sleep.

Voices woke him, and when he opened his eyes, it was almost dark. He glanced up at the window and saw the purple and orange rays of sunset starting to darken.

He listened, trying to identify the speakers, but the conversation sounded as if it were being conducted in near whispers. Then, the unmistakable lilt of Samantha McCrae rose above the muttering. "I don't see why we're standing here arguing, Sheriff."

"I'm not arguing with the two of you, damnit, I just want you to understand what you're doing," Hansen said, his own voice rising in irritation.

"Damn it, Merrill, I'm not a fool. I know what I'm doing. Now come on, open the door. You got the order from Judge Lassiter. You want to argue with him about it, go right ahead, but I want Slocum out of that cell right now." Dan McCrae sounded as if he were no less angry than Sheriff Hansen.

Slocum sat on the edge of the cot, his eyes fixed on the door to the outer office. Finally, he saw Hansen's face float into view behind the grate. The office was lit by lamplight now, and the hollows of Hansen's face were filled with shadows that made him look almost sinister.

The door swung back, and Merrill Hansen stepped through, glared at him, then turned to wave Dan McCrae into the cell block.

McCrae stepped to the cell door, then turned and gestured impatiently for Hansen. "Come on, Merrill, open it up."

Hansen hefted the thick iron key ring, filling the cell block with a noisy jangle. He was moving slowly, and it was apparent that he was not happy about being forced to release his prisoner. He inserted the key into the lock, then stopped. He let his hand fall, and turned to McCrae. "Dan, you know I think this is a bad idea."

"I know what you think, Merrill, but Slocum didn't kill that boy. Or Dalton either."

"I got witnesses, Dan. Three of 'em. And they say different."

"I don't give a damn what they say, Merrill. They're wrong or they're flat out lying. Either way, Slocum don't belong in jail. His bail's been paid, and that's that."

Hansen nodded, turned back to the door, and turned the key. He stayed in front of the door for a long moment, as if somewhere in the back of his mind was that thought that if he didn't move, then Slocum wouldn't have to be released. Slocum stepped to the cell door, put both hands on the bars, and waited patiently.

Finally, McCrae took the sheriff by the shoulder and tugged him aside none too gently. "Come on, Merrill, you're wasting time."

Slocum pushed the door open and followed McCrae out of the cell block. Hansen closed the cell door and brought up the rear.

In the office, Slocum sat down across from Hansen's desk. The sheriff seemed surprised, moved around behind the desk and lowered himself carefully into his own chair.

"I would've thought you'd want to be out of here in a hurry, Slocum," he said.

"I want to know who your witnesses are, Sheriff."

"You plan to bushwhack them too, do you?"

"You got no call to talk like that, Merrill," McCrae snapped. He started to say more, but Slocum stopped him with a raised hand.

"Sheriff Hansen's only doing his job, Mr. McCrae. He's wrong, but you can't blame him for that. I don't know that I'd do anything different, under the circumstances."

"You can afford to be tolerant, John, but I don't think it's the best way to get to the bottom of this. Give him the names, Merrill."

Hansen sucked on his lower lip for a moment. "I know I got to do it. And I reckon you got a right to know. But I want to tell you one thing, Slocum. And you listen to me real good, now. Anything happens to any of these men, I will come looking for you. Understand what I'm sayin'?"

"I understand," Slocum said.

"All right, then. Dave Duncan, Doak Henry, and Bobby Pietras. That's who says you're the one who done it. Now, you remember what I said. You better hope they don't get sick, or have an accident. They even get hit by lightning, I'm gonna throw you back in that cell so fast your head will spin."

"Fair enough."

"Stay away from them, Slocum."

"Can't promise that, Sheriff. I have to try to find out why they want to frame me."

"You heard what I said."

"Yeah, I heard you."

17

On the way back to the Double Deuce, Slocum kept looking over his shoulder. He wasn't sure why, but he at least half-expected that someone, maybe Meyer, maybe one of the men who had claimed they had witnessed the murder of Ray and Timmy Dalton, would be following him.

But the road was deserted. Samantha kept drifting toward him and, with her father there, it made Slocum uncomfortable. Dan McCrae continued to stare straight ahead, as if he were alone on the road, and Slocum wondered what was going through the rancher's mind.

By the time they reached the lane leading up the hill to the house, Slocum knew what he had to do, and he wondered whether he had a chance in hell of pulling it off. But first he wanted to settle things with Dan McCrae. The rancher dismounted, then climbed the steps. Only when he reached the door on the front gallery did he stop and look at Slocum. "You coming in or not?" he asked.

Slocum nodded, and he started up the steps with Samantha right behind him. McCrae led the way into his study, moved behind his desk and sat down. Slocum sat on a leather chair, and Samantha stood in the doorway.

You'd best leave us alone, Sam." McCrae said. "We got some things to discuss."

"You keep shooing me away," she said. It wasn't a whine, just a statement, matter-of-factly delivered, but with enough steel in it to suggest that she would not be shooed away again. "I want to know what's going to happen. I have a right to know."

McCrae puffed his cheeks, rubbed his forehead, then leaned back in his chair. "I guess you do," he said. "Come in and close the door."

Samantha stepped through the doorway, closed the heavy walnut door and stood there for a long moment, her back to the men. It looked to Slocum as if she were trying to decide whether the threshold she had just crossed was one she would regret. Her head nodded, as if to acknowledge some words he hadn't heard. The movement sent ripples of sheet lightning shimmering through her long black hair. Then she turned around and walked to the desk.

Sitting on one corner, she slid back to gain a secure purchase, then folded her hands in her lap. "Go ahead," she said, "talk."

"Thanks for bailing me out, Mr. McCrae," Slocum said. "It must have cost you a lot of money."

McCrae, sucking on the inside of his cheek, shook his head. "Don't worry about it. I can afford it, John."

"I know that, but I appreciate it all the same."

"I think you'd best pack up and move on, John."

Slocum shook his head. "No, sir. I can't do that."

"Why not?"

"First off, I can't let you lose the money for my bail. And more important than that, I can't run, leaving people thinking I killed that boy. I didn't do it and I intend to prove it."

"John, nobody thinks you did it. Least nobody whose opinion is worth a spit. Just go. It ain't running, either. It's just common sense. Folks won't think you're a coward if you leave, but they'll think you a fool if you stay. You can count on that."

"I'm neither."

"I know that, but what do you think you can accomplish by staying? What is there to prove?"

"You know the answer to that, Dan."

McCrae took a deep breath and held it for a long time. When he finally exhaled, he seemed to have come to some sort of conclusion, which he signified by nodding his head. "All right," he said, "what do you want me to do?"

"Nothing. I'll handle it. Cord Meyer is behind this, and I intend to find the proof."

"He'll kill you," Samantha said. "Daddy's right. You should leave."

"He won't kill me, Miss McCrae. Not unless I make a mistake."

"Suppose you do?"

"I won't."

She chewed on her lower lip, but said nothing.

McCrae leaned forward. "You'll need a place to stay. Someplace where you'll be safe, someplace no one will think to look for you."

"I've slept on the open range before. It's not a problem."

"But we won't know where to find you if we have to. It's better if there's someplace we know about. Even if you just check in every couple of days, at least it's better than not knowing where the hell you are. If you're here, you won't get anything done, so . . ." He snapped his fingers. "I know the just the place. There's an old line shack, in the hills toward Rock Falls Canyon." He tapped Samantha on the hip. "You know where it is, Sam, don't you?"

She nodded. "You mean the place I used to hide when I'd run away?"

"That's the one. You and Slocum pack some grub for him. Enough to last a few days."

"I can take him there," Samantha said.

"No, I don't want you out there alone."

"I'll be all right, Daddy."

"Suppose somebody is waiting for John? If they are, you might get hurt."

"We'll go after dark. Nobody will see us. If you keep the men busy, it'll work. I know it will."

"I don't know. I think—"

"It's the best way, and you know it, Daddy."

McCrae agreed, but his heart wasn't in it. "All right," he sighed. "Do it your way."

"Ben could come with us, if it'll make you feel better."

"No," McCrae said. "I don't want anybody but the three of us in this room to know where Slocum is staying. As far as Bracken is concerned, he left this evening, he's gone, and he's not coming back."

"That's it, then," Samantha said. She slid off the desk. "I'll get some food ready." She walked to the door, opened it, and slipped through, then pulled it shut behind her.

Slocum sat there feeling as if his life were beyond his control. People were making decisions that determined his future, and he seemed to have nothing to say about it. The fact is, he thought, I *don't* have anything to say about it.

"Anything else we ought to consider?" Dan McCrae asked.

When Slocum shook his head, the rancher stood and walked to an oak cabinet in a corner of the room. He opened the locked door with a key from his watch chain. Slocum couldn't see what was in the cabinet, but when McCrae turned around, he was holding a Spencer buffalo gun. "I believe in fighting fire with fire," he said. "You take this."

Slocum got to his feet and walked to the corner, where he accepted the heavy rifle. Freed of its weight, McCrae reached back into the cabinet for a box of shells. He thrust them at the surprised cowboy, a slight grin tugging at the corners of his mouth. "You get the goods on

Meyer," he said, "you'll need this. It'll stop anything on earth. Ever use one?"

"Once," Slocum said. "And my shoulder's *still* sore."

"We better find Sam," McCrae said. "You take care of that girl, Slocum. I don't know what the two of you are up to together, and it's none of my business. She's old enough to know her own mind and she wouldn't listen to me even if she weren't. Just like her mother. But don't you hurt her. You understand?"

Slocum nodded. He stuck out his hand, and McCrae gripped it firmly. Then, just to reinforce his point, he squeezed, enough for Slocum to realize just how powerful a man Dan McCrae was.

The rancher led the way out of his study. They found Samantha in the kitchen, just drawing the string on a canvas bag. Without looking at either of them, she said, "There's beans, coffee, flour, bacon, and some dried beef. Enough for a few days, if you're careful. I'll bring more later. We'd better go."

"Give me a few minutes," McCrae said. "I'll go over to the bunkhouse, and make sure there's nobody around." He left through the rear door.

Samantha looked at Slocum, gnawed her lower lip, but said nothing. A clock on the wall in the dining room clicked louder and louder, filling the room with its insistent rhythm. Suddenly the gears whirred, and a chime started to toll. It stopped at nine, and Samantha said, "We'd better go."

Slocum took the sack and headed for the hallway. He grabbed the Spencer as he passed the study doorway, and Sam took the box of .50 shells. It was dark when they stepped out onto the porch. Crickets chirred and clacked in the tall grass, and, off in the distance, an uncertain owl hooted twice.

They left the porch and climbed into their saddles without speaking. Samantha led the way down the lane, the canvas bag a dark lump at the back of her saddle, and Slocum looked back at the big, white house, wondering if he'd ever see it again. When they reached the far end of the lane, the house was just a bulky shadow atop the hill, lights burning in two windows like the orange eyes of a black cat. He had the Spencer cradled across his thighs, and its weight kept reminding him of what might lie ahead.

There would be a moon later on, but for the time being, they had to rely on what little light there was, the horses picking their way carefully, not hesitant, but reluctant to run flat out. Their hooves thudded on the thick turf like muffled drums. It was nearly two hours before the moon finally appeared, at first peeking reluctantly over the horizon, then suddenly exploding into a huge silver disc. The wash of moonlight coated everything with a tarnished silvery glow, but made their journey easier.

An hour later they could see the line shack, its weathered wood giving it the appearance of ancient pewter under the moon. Slocum dismounted and opened the door, sweeping away a spiderweb with one hand as he pushed inside. Samantha was right behind him, the canvas bag wrapped in her arms. "There should be a lamp," she said.

Slocum lit a match, then searched around in the musty-smelling crevices until he saw the dusty lamp, its chimney grimed over and tacked to the wall with another spiderweb. The match guttered out, and Slocum lit another, lifted the chimney and applied the flame to the wick. The reservoir was nearly full and the wick caught after a few seconds, filling the shack with wan copper light.

"What a mess," Samantha said, dropping the bag and looking around. "It'll take hours to clean it up." She walked to the far wall, where a cot was attached to the wall. She lifted a dusty sheet, tugged it away, and rolled it into a ball. Coughing because of the dust, she sat on the cot.

"You better get back, Sam," Slocum said, blowing a layer of dust from the rickety table which, with a pair of no less rickety chairs, completed the inventory of furniture.

"I'll go back in the morning," she said.

"Your father will worry," Slocum said.

"Daddy's a big boy, and he knows I'm a big girl. Besides, first things first." She started unbuttoning her denim shirt. Before Slocum could object, she yanked it open. Her pale skin looked bronze in the lamplight as she stood up, tossed the shirt at him, and bent over to tug off her boots.

"Sam, I . . ."

"I know what you're going to say, because you're a gentleman. And it's nice, but it's irrelevant. I know what I want, John." She unbuckled her jeans, wriggled out of them, stepped out away from the pile of denim, and held out her arms. "Come here," she said.

Slocum turned and walked to the door. She thought for a second he was going to leave, but he just closed the door and turned to look at her. Naked, every curve seemed to gleam in the lamplight. Head to foot, her body was as perfect as any he'd ever seen. He undressed quickly and walked to her, already growing erect.

"Eager, aren't you," she said, winking. She reached out and took him in her hand, stroking him until he was hard. Letting him go, she backed up a couple of steps, felt the edge of the cot against her calves, and sat down, then lay back, stretching her arms over her head.

He moved closer, then knelt by the cot. Her eyes were closed, her lips slightly parted, and he saw her tongue flick out, moisten them, then disappear. Leaning over, he kissed her gently, felt her tongue suddenly dart into his mouth and withdraw. "I hope you're not going to be disappointed," he said, bending to take one erect nipple in his mouth. She said nothing, but her body quivered and he realized she was shaking her head to tell him she wouldn't be.

Letting the nipple slide from between his lips, he traced the curve of a rib with the tip of his tongue. The dampness he left behind glistened in the lamplight as he went lower, flicking his tongue into her navel then burying his face in the dark mass of curls between her legs. She turned slightly, up on one hip, and bent her right leg at the knee. He could smell the musk of her, and small opals trembled on the lowest curls. One by one he drew them into his mouth as her body began to tremble and she pushed his head lower. The thick flesh of her, salty and dark, slid across his lips as his tongue began to probe into her. He could hear her breathing, shallow gasps punctuated by the sharp hissing of sudden inhalations. Taking her thighs in his hands, he pressed her legs wide open and lapped hungrily, until her juices dampened the mattress ticking beneath her and her thighs shone with a coppery gleam.

Shifting his weight, he brought one leg onto the cot, then raised his head. He looked at her. Her eyes were still closed, her head thrown back and her lips parted, her tongue curled in one corner. Kneeling between her legs, he held his erection in one hand as, sensing him so close, Samantha raised her hips. He rubbed the head of his cock against the swollen lips, his fingers stroking her bush for a moment until, with a sudden thrust, he slid inside her. Her legs curled around him, and she opened her eyes to stare into his as he started to rock, slowly at first, then faster as he drove all the way home and tried to find her rhythm.

"It's about time," she whispered, reaching out to him. He leaned forward, supporting himself now on his elbows, feeling her breasts flatten against his chest.

18

Slocum stood in front of the line shack, watching Samantha ride toward the rising sun. He stood there for a long time, until the huge, red ball first reduced her to a dark smear on its surface, then swallowed her altogether.

Once she was out of sight, he set to work. There was much to do, and he hardly knew where to begin. He wanted to find Cord Meyer, thinking that the regulator was both the beginning and the end of the problem. There might be, he well knew, a long way to travel between those points, but it was time to begin.

He cleaned and loaded the Spencer, tucked some rations into his saddlebags, along with the box of .50 caliber shells, and mounted his horse. The chestnut seemed to sense that something important was happening, and was so frisky Slocum had his hands full for the first half mile.

He knew that Meyer could be anywhere out there in the hundreds of square miles between him and the Double Deuce, but two things were clear—Meyer was interested in fomenting as much trouble as he could between the cattlemen and the sheepherders, and Dave Duncan, for whatever reason, had thrown in with the regulator. Maybe it was as simple a thing as jealousy over Samantha McCrae, and maybe it was so complicated a thing that Duncan himself couldn't explain his reasons if you held a gun to his head.

But Slocum was betting that if he could find Dave Duncan, sooner or later the cowhand would lead him to the regulator. And he knew that the supposed witnesses, Duncan included, were in some jeopardy. If Meyer was behind the frame, he wouldn't want to run the risk of having it fall apart because one of the perjurers suddenly felt a chill below his ankles.

And Slocum was certain that Meyer would not let things drag on to a trial. He'd want Slocum dead if he could find him and, failing that, would make sure the witnesses didn't live long enough to recant. Kill them, Meyer would think, and he would tighten the noose around Slocum's neck. It was not for nothing that Merrill Hansen had warned Slocum that he would be the first man the sheriff would look for if anything happened to Duncan, Pietras, or Henry.

Duncan was the key, that much seemed clear. It was all beginning to fall into place as he sifted through what he knew and what he could guess. Duncan had left the Double Deuce for the Broken A, he was a witness against Slocum, and he had been the man sent to recover Slocum's Winchester from Rock Falls Canyon. He hadn't found it, or at least had said he hadn't, yet Merrill Hansen had the rifle and claimed it was used to kill an innocent man and his blameless child.

It now seemed clear that Duncan must have found the rifle and kept that fact secret for purposes that were now beginning to come clear. And it had been Doak Henry who told Duncan that Slocum had something going with Samantha, so Dave Duncan might not have been the first defector to the regulator's side. Meyer was there in the background, but there were layers of protection between him and Slocum, like the layers of an onion protecting the heart. But onions could be peeled.

Slocum made tracks for the Broken A. He would have to be careful because the men at Ramsey's place would have itchy trigger fingers. The chance to take Slocum down would be tempting and, if Duncan or Henry were there to incite the others, even likely.

Two hours later, Slocum was on Broken A land. It was a big spread, not as large as the Double Deuce, but almost, and it lay on the far side of Ray Dalton's small place. So far there was no sign of any of the hands. Unlike Dan McCrae, Frank Ramsey was not interested in fence. He wanted his herds to run free, to chew on open range grass to their hearts' content. He would round them up and sell them without the cost of fence and the distracting labor of stringing wire.

But the hands would be out with the herds. Since the slaughter of the beeves had begun, no one wanted to take the chance of losing any more cattle, so the hands were camping on the range, close enough to keep an eye on the steers or to hear the click of a cocked hammer should the butcher decide to strike again.

Far ahead, breaking over a rise, a huge herd of cattle shambled along, grazing and bellowing, sweeping like a reluctant wave over the hillside. Somewhere nearby, Slocum knew, would be some of the Broken A crew, maybe Duncan among them. So far as he knew, Pietras and Henry were still working for McCrae, but that could change in a hurry.

Slocum backed off a little, dismounted, and tugged the chestnut back below the crest of the ridge on which he sat, then, taking binoculars from his saddlebag, crept back to the top of the ridge. He lay on his stomach and crawled the last few yards, parting the grass with one hand to give himself a decent view of the far hillside. He ripped a couple of handfuls of the long grass and gripped the field glasses with them, trying to cut down on the chance of a glint from the lenses tipping off his presence.

Looking through the binoculars, he traced the ridgeline from left to right. The cows were still coming, and their muted bellowing was a steady grumble, filling the valley below with the sound of an approaching thunderstorm. He spotted the first Stetson then, as an outrider far to the left bobbed up over the ridge.

Slocum adjusted the focus, trying to get a clear look at the cowhand. The face looked only vaguely familiar, and he guessed it was someone he had seen in Bracken at one of the saloons. But it wasn't Dave Duncan. Sweeping the glasses slowly to the right, he saw nothing but cattle until he got to the other side of the herd. Two more men, riding side by side and busy chewing the fat, drifted with the outer edge of the cattle. He didn't know either man.

Since the hands were there for protection and not driving the herd, there was no point man. There was no need. And it looked like easy duty. All the men had to do was stay in the saddle and stay alert. It sure as hell beat running wire, and Slocum found himself wondering whether that had been the real reason for Dave Duncan's sudden move to the Broken A.

The tail end of the herd started to come into view as the bulk of the cattle streamed downhill like a spreading stain. The rear ranks were thin already and growing thinner. Here and there, patches of trampled yellow-green were visible among the brown clusters where the steers in tens and twelves huddled together as they munched their way sidewise down the slope.

And finally, bringing up the rear, three more men appeared on the hilltop. One by one, Slocum checked them out. The third was Dave Duncan. The kid's round, still peach-fuzzed cheeks, the sparse beard sun-bleached almost white against the bronzed shin, was unmistakable.

The bulk of the herd had reached the broad valley floor now, and seemed to be settling in for a long stay. There was plenty of grass and, in a jagged line across the floor, clumps of rushes and brush where a shallow brook wound from northwest to southeast. The growth on both sides was lush and too thick for the water to be seen, but Slocum knew it was there, and so did the cattle. The front ranks of the herd had slowed considerably, and had stopped altogether in some places as the last of the steers reached the valley floor.

Slocum watched as the hands gathered in a clump, still on horseback, at the edge of the creek. All but one of them dismounted. The last man drifted slowly away, and Slocum trained the glasses on him to be sure, but knew even before the binoculars were in focus that it was Dave Duncan.

The kid was heading northwest, staying close to the creek, and following its meandering course. He didn't seem to be in any hurry, letting his roan set the pace at a canter. On the off chance that Duncan had a rendezvous, Slocum scanned the northern end of the valley, but saw nothing to indicate that anyone was waiting for the kid.

He followed the young hand with the glasses until Duncan started uphill, then he slithered backward through the grass and untethered the chestnut. He tugged the horse a few steps further downhill before swinging into the saddle. Keeping below the ridgeline, he headed north. Watching the ridge, he was ready to rein in at the first sign of Duncan. But it now looked like the kid was going to ride right out of the valley's north end.

Slocum had gone more than a mile before Duncan's hat bobbed above the ridge for a split second, disappeared, then popped up again. Apparently, Duncan was running parallel to the ridge, a few yards below the crest. The chestnut was running hard, and Slocum had considerably narrowed the gap between him and Duncan, closed it enough, he thought, to take the chance of dismounting and running up to the crest to get a better look.

Slocum dismounted, raced to the crest, field glasses in hand, and looked for Duncan. He was taking a chance, because he had to expose himself to the rest of the Broken A crew in order to get a good look at Duncan, but it couldn't be helped.

The cowboy was very close to the end of the valley now, high on the ridge and dead ahead of Slocum. A cursory sweep of the field glasses gave no hint of Duncan's purpose. There wasn't a sign of another man, and Slocum had no choice but to clamber back down to the chestnut and resume his pursuit.

Goading the horse with his spurs, Slocum forced the chestnut into a gallop. The stallion responded with a burst of speed on the tricky footing. The ridge was still angling uphill, but more gently, and there was less than a mile to the point where it peaked, then broke sharply downhill into the next valley.

Slocum still caught glimpses of Duncan's Stetson as the kid stayed on course, now less than a quarter mile away. When Duncan reached the peak, he disappeared on the far side as abruptly as a man falling off a cliff, and Slocum pushed the stallion even harder.

He knew he ran the risk of riding right up Duncan's back, but he had no choice. Approaching the razor-backed peak, he slowed, then eased the chestnut forward at a walk. Glasses in hand, he reined in and moved forward cautiously. Then, when he was within thirty yards of the peak, he dismounted once more and sprinted forward until he could see down into the next valley.

He saw Duncan right away, still riding flat out. Far below, a small lake glittered with sunlight. On its wind-rippled surface he could see the sun reflected, and several clouds drifted across it almost as if they were in the water below. The effect was that of looking through a hole in the earth to another sun on the opposite side.

And on the far side, a solitary man sat on the shore, a black horse behind him. Using the glasses, Slocum zeroed in and picked out the face of the man—it was Doak Henry. Henry was not looking up toward him, but Slocum could see his features clearly in the tranquil surface of the water at the shoreline.

It was more than a mile to where Henry sat, trailing a single stalk of Indian paintbrush in the muddy sand at the water's edge. But that was as the crow flies, and Duncan would have to skirt the edge of the lake and add nearly a half mile to the distance. Slocum didn't have much of a chance getting there on horseback without being seen, but he knew he couldn't pass up the chance to get to Duncan. Even if he had to hold him at gunpoint, he had to talk to the kid; he'd pick his brains if Duncan were on the square, and threaten to pistol-whip him if he weren't.

Slocum raced back to the chestnut, hobbled the horse, then grabbed the Spencer and a handful of shells for it. Breaking into a run, he headed back the way he'd come and started down into the valley. What cover there was was sparse, confined to clumps of brush and scattered clusters of boulders seeming to float on the lush grass like gray corks on a green sea.

The thickness of the grass hampered him a bit, but if he were going to get there at all, it would have to be on foot. If he were to charge downhill on horseback, the best he could hope for was that he would spook his quarry, and at the worst he'd be asking for a gunfight. If he had to kill the men, they'd tell him nothing. And if they killed him . . . well. . . .

He could see Duncan, the roan backed off to a walk beneath him, angling to the far side of the lake. Apparently he hadn't seen Henry or, if he had, he was in no hurry to get to him. That gave Slocum time he desperately needed.

He was already feeling the effects of his breathless plunge downhill, and his heart hammered in his chest. His throat felt as if it had been coated with sand, and his side burned as if someone had slit it open with a white-hot blade. But he kept on running.

Doak Henry had seen Duncan now and gotten to his feet. He stood there watching Duncan across the water, hands on hips, the stem of the paintbrush now clamped between his teeth. Slocum was only a hundred yards away from the last cluster of boulders and another seventy from Henry's horse.

He reached the boulders and half fell behind them, where he lay panting. Peering out from behind the rocks, Slocum watched as Duncan approached. The former Double Deuce hand was still two hundred yards from Henry when the latter yelled, "Where in the hell have you been, Dunc?"

Duncan yelled back, but Slocum couldn't make out the words. Slocum gulped air into his burning lungs as he waited for Duncan to arrive. If he could get the drop on the cowboys, he just might be able to force them to talk to him. He crossed his fingers and kept on panting, waiting for Duncan to cover the last fifty yards.

He brought the Spencer around and trained it on Henry. Over the sights, he watched as Duncan dismounted and walked the last twenty yards. The men had already begun to talk, but they were close enough that they had no need to raise their voices, and it was difficult to hear what they were saying. Slocum wished he could hear just a bit better. He might learn something useful, maybe get a lever he could use to pry something out of Duncan, something he could use to nail Cord Meyer.

Slithering through the grass, pushing the Spencer ahead of him, he tried to narrow the gap. There was some scattered brush, but it was sparse and little of it reached more than three feet in height, but it would have to do.

Keeping his eye on the two cowhands, he eased closer. Their voices were clearer now, but still not clear enough. Slocum eased ahead another five yards and lay still.

Then Dave Duncan's head exploded into a red mist and a hail of bone. The boom of a buffalo gun rolled across the valley floor, a single thunderous handclap that shattered into a dozen feeble imitations before it slowly died away.

19

Doak Henry screamed. Slocum saw the cowboy kneel beside Duncan's nearly headless body, then, as if trying to comprehend what had happened, look slowly around. Slocum, knowing Henry was next, scrambled to his feet and charged ahead. Henry seemed not to hear him until the last second. He was starting to turn as Slocum hurled himself through the air, planting his right shoulder in the middle of Henry's back and knocking him down.

Henry struggled free, dragging himself out from under Slocum's weight. He grabbed Slocum by the shoulder and got to his knees then scrambled to his feet.

"Get down," Slocum shouted.

Henry stared at him, frozen for a moment, and Slocum tackled him. A slug whistled overhead and a moment later the boom of the big buffalo gun filtered down into the valley.

"Let me go," Henry shouted, still trying to get free. But Slocum held on. Henry reached for his Colt but Slocum knocked it loose just as it cleared the holster.

145

"Listen to me," Slocum shouted. "Do you want to end up like Duncan?"

Henry seemed stunned by the question. But he started to get to his knees again, and once more Slocum hauled him down.

"Get down and stay down, Henry," Slocum barked. He drew his own pistol and leveled it at the confused cowhand. "Don't you understand what's happening here?" Slocum asked.

Henry's jaw went slack. A moment later, his head shook slowly from side to side. "No, no I don't. I don't understand."

"Meyer's trying to kill you, Doak." Slocum said. Henry looked around as if he expected to see the regulator standing right behind him.

"You can't see him, Doak. He's too far away for that. He's using a Sharps, and he'll take your head off the next time you stand up. Just like he did Duncan's. Is that what you want?"

Once more, the confused cowhand shook his head dumbly. He seemed almost to be in a state of shock. His lips trembled then, and he said, "His head . . . Dunc's head . . . it blew up. Oh my God." He started to cry then, burying his face in his hands. Slocum squirmed through the grass until he could reach out and press Henry flat.

His hand came away sticky. It was speckled with blood and bits of brain tissue. One sliver of bone gleamed like ivory in the sunlight. Closing his eyes, Slocum wiped his hand in the grass. He could feel the dust and seed hulls clinging to his skin, and he scraped again and again until it felt smooth. Turning the palm up and opening his eyes again, he saw the dark, congealed rings left behind by Duncan's blood.

"You feel betrayed, don't you, Doak?"

Henry didn't answer him, but Slocum pushed on. "You were helping him. You lied to Sheriff Hansen about me, and now Meyer's trying to kill you before you can change your story. You understand that, don't you? You know that's what's happening, what happened to Duncan and what will happen to you and Pietras?"

Henry groaned. He rolled onto his back, still covering his face with his hands. "It wasn't supposed to be like this."

"Ray Dalton is dead, Doak. And an eleven-year-old boy is dead. Who in hell do you think killed them?"

"I didn't have anything to do with that."

"But Meyer did. You must know that now."

Henry shook his head, still keeping his hands clamped over his face. Slocum backed off and watched the kid for a moment. His shirt was splattered with blood and lumps of gray pulp, and a piece of bone was stuck in Henry's chest. The cowhand's own blood seeped through the shirt around the bone and Slocum reached out to grab the splinter between his fingers and jerk it free.

The kid twitched, but never moved his hands. "They were already dead when we got there. We heard the shooting and we come over to see what happened," he mumbled.

"And Meyer was already there?"

Henry nodded. "Yeah, he was there. He said he knew you done it, that he'd seen you and that it was a chance for Dunc to get even with you, get you out of circulation and keep you away from Sam McCrae."

"We figured we owed Dunc. He was a friend so . . ."

"And Duncan had my Winchester, did he?"

Once more, Henry nodded. "Yeah. He give it to Meyer. Meyer said it would make sure the sheriff believed you killed Dalton and his kid."

"It did that, all right. But you know who really killed them, don't you? Now?"

"Meyer, I guess. I mean . . ."

"Where's Pietras?"

"Supposed to meet us at Rock Falls Canyon. We was all goin' there. Meyer, too. Pietras was supposed to come with Dunc, but he got held up, so he was gonna meet us there later."

Slocum took a deep breath. "You know what we have to do, don't you?"

Henry shook his head.

"We have to get there first, or Bobby Pietras is a dead man."

"How? How the hell can we leave here? We can't get—"

"It's the only chance we have. Meyer probably thinks he got you and Duncan."

"Then let's go," Henry said, removing his hands and looking at Slocum for the first time. "We can't let him kill Bobby . . ."

"We have to make sure he's gone, first."

"But—"

"You want to be the one sticks his head up to see, Doak? Do you?"

Henry shook his head. He coughed back a sob, then looked at his shirt. He brushed it with his hands. Only then did he realize what had soiled it. "My God . . ." he said, then rolled over and vomited into the grass.

Slocum heard something up on the ridge and looked up toward where he had left the chestnut. Three riders were just coming over the ridge. He realized that the Broken A crew must have heard the gunshots and sent someone to see what was happening.

Slocum wanted to jump up and wave his arms, but Meyer was still out there somewhere, and he couldn't take the chance.

"Riders coming, Doak," he told Henry.

Henry started to sit up, but Slocum held him down. "Don't!" he said.

"We have to let them know where we are," Henry argued.

"You could be letting Meyer know, too," Slocum reminded him.

"We have to warn them!"

"Meyer doesn't care about them, Doak. He wanted you and Duncan, that's all. And Pietras."

Doak nodded as if he understood. "And you," he said.

"If he gets you and Pietras, he's got me, Doak. There'll be no one left to tell Hansen what happened to Ray Dalton and his boy. That's good enough for Meyer."

The two men lay there, watching the three riders ease their way down the hill. Despite what he'd just told Henry, Slocum wasn't sure whether Meyer would open fire on them. He wasn't even sure that Meyer was still out there. All he knew for certain was that the clock was ticking for Bobby Pietras. And there was only one way to save him—get to Cord Meyer first.

Slocum waited impatiently for the three Broken A hands. He suddenly realized that matters were more complicated than he'd thought. He was going to have to get them to believe his story and to take Doak back to Bracken to tell Merrill Hansen the truth. Under no circumstances could he afford to let Henry accompany him in his pursuit of Meyer, because if he got to the regulator too late to save Pietras, Henry would be the only one left to tell the truth.

And he wasn't willing to let Henry go back alone. Meyer could be anywhere, and until he was under lock and key, or better yet under six feet of sandy soil, Henry was a walking target for the regulator's big Sharps.

Cupping his hands to his mouth, Slocum shouted to the riders. One of them seemed to have heard something. He reined in and held up a hand. The other two had drifted on downhill until the first man shouted something to them. They pulled up, and Slocum shouted again, this time with Henry joining him.

One of the men spotted the waving arms as Henry snapped a kerchief back and forth above the grass. Abruptly, the three riders plunged downhill, now heading straight for Slocum and Henry.

Slocum made sure the Spencer was loaded and then whipped the field glasses from around his neck and scanned the high ground in every direction. There wasn't a trace of Meyer, but he wasn't surprised. The regulator seemed adept at ambush, and probably had chosen his cover well and in advance. If he was still there, there would be no way to know until the Sharps sent another thunderclap rolling across the valley. But by then, the bullet would long since have found its target.

The riders were on the valley floor now, skirting the edge of the lake as they galloped toward the two prostrate men. Four minutes later, they were pulling up not ten yards from Duncan's corpse. One of the riders pulled his handgun and pointed it at Slocum "You bastard," he shouted.

"Wait," Henry screamed. "Don't shoot!"

The man leaped from the saddle and sprinted toward Slocum. He thumbed back the hammer, but Henry shouted again, "Wait! Damn you, Donny, put it up!"

Donny Comfort seemed bewildered. He kept the Colt trained on Slocum, and his finger was still curled around the trigger, but he was looking at Doak Henry. "What the hell's going on," he demanded.

"Cord Meyer just killed Duncan," Slocum told him.

"Bullshit!"

"It's true, Donny," Henry said. "It wasn't Slocum. It was Meyer."

"Why in hell would he kill Duncan? They're on the same side. We all are . . ." and he waved the pistol in Slocum's direction, "except for you."

"Meyer only has one side, Donny—his own," Slocum said. "It's complicated, and there's no time to fill you in now. You've got to get Doak to Sheriff Hansen."

"Why?"

"Slocum never killed the Daltons," Henry said.

"Then who did? Meyer?" Comfort looked skeptical, but he waited for Henry's answer.

"I think so. Dalton was already dead when we got there, and Meyer was already there. We never even seen Slocum that day. But Dunc wanted to get even with Slocum, and Meyer had the idea to pin the killing on him."

"Look," Slocum said. "Doak can tell you all about it on the way into Bracken. I've got to go."

"The hell you do," Comfort said. He waved the pistol threateningly.

But Henry shook his head. "Meyer's gonna kill Bobby," he said. "Let Slocum go."

"Why don't we all go?" Comfort said, still skeptical, but lowering the hammer on his Colt.

"Because I'm the only one who can go head to head with him," Slocum said, hefting the Spencer. "You'll never get close enough. And somebody's got to make sure Doak, here, stays alive long enough to tell Hansen what really happened."

"But—"

"No, Donny. There's no time. Meyer knows where Pietras is and he's probably already on the way. You have to protect Henry."

Doak started to get up, and Slocum once more held him down. To Comfort, he said, "Bring the horses over here."

Comfort called to the other two hands who were kneeling by Duncan's body. "Jake, you and Billy bring your mounts over here. Bring mine, and Doak's, too."

When the horses were in position, Slocum told Henry to use them to cover himself. Henry crawled in among them and got to his feet. "You better walk them up the hill," Slocum said. "And don't let Henry in the saddle until you cross the ridge." He told them where the chestnut was, and asked them to pick it up and bring it to the Double Deuce. He would use Duncan's roan.

"And where the hell are you going, Slocum?" Comfort asked.

"Where the hell do you think?"

20

There was no time for trailcraft. Slocum had to ride hell for leather and hope that he beat Meyer to Rock Falls Canyon. There was the risk that Meyer would spot him, but it was a chance he had to take. If he took a long route, Meyer would certainly beat him there, and that would seal the fate of Bobby Pietras.

Duncan's roan was broad shouldered and long legged. The big stallion was uneasy with a stranger on his back, but he gave Slocum no trouble when he felt the spurs digging into his flanks. He ran flat out, and kept on running with just an occasional prod.

Slocum kept his eyes peeled for the regulator, but after an hour, there was still no sign of Meyer, not even a telltale cloud of dust drifting across the hills on the slight breeze. It was hot, and the sun was hammering his back. Sweat trickled down between his shoulder blades and dampened his shirt in sticky patches. He was thirsty, and drank on the fly, polishing off the last few sips of water in Duncan's canteen when he still had a half hour's ride ahead of him.

But thirst was the least of his worries. Nagging at the back of his mind was the possibility that Doak Henry would refuse to tell Hansen what he knew, and as Slocum thought about it, he realized that Henry had nothing to lose by keeping his mouth shut. The cowboy had to consider the possibility that it would be Meyer, not Slocum, who would walk out of Rock Falls Canyon. And if that were to be the case, the last thing Doak Henry would want would be to have to face Cord Meyer's thirst for revenge. It would be better to sit on his hands and wait—if Slocum came out on top, there would be plenty of time to set Hansen straight.

It was early afternoon by the time the narrow mouth of the canyon came into view. The sun was ahead of Slocum now, its rays slanting down into his face and causing him to squint to see the details on the rock face on either side of the canyon mouth.

The creek glistened like a band of burnished silver where it gushed through the opening, flattened out, then wound across the valley floor. It was painful to look at, and Slocum kept his eyes fixed high on the cliff, looking for some hint of Meyer's presence. There was none, but he kept on looking.

Pietras was almost certainly at the canyon mouth or inside. And Meyer would have his choice of going in to take care of Pietras at close range or riding up to the top of the mesa and using the Sharps from the rimrock. Either way, Pietras would never know what hit him. He had no reason to fear Meyer or to suspect that his life was in danger. As far as he knew, four men were going to meet and plan their next step. But Meyer had already made plans of his own, and there was no room in them for Bobby Pietras.

Closing on the canyon mouth, Slocum slowed the roan to a walk the last two hundred yards. At fifty, he reined in, slipped out of the saddle and tethered the roan to a scrub oak. Taking the Spencer and checking his pocket for extra shells, he sprinted toward the creek and waded across to the north side. The Spencer was heavy and he wondered whether he'd have been better off with Duncan's carbine. But when he thought of Meyer's long range marksmanship, he realized the Springfield in Duncan's boot was just no match for the big buffalo rifle.

Sprinting along the creek toward the mouth of the canyon, he tried to keep one eye on the rim and the other on the interior of the small stone box. Reaching the base of the wall on the north side, he flattened his back against it and paused to listen. He didn't expect to hear anything, and he didn't.

Staying against the wall, he looked over his left shoulder along the base of the mesa face. Twenty yards away, he saw what looked like the foot of a narrow trail. It appeared to lead in a zig-zag path up the face of the wall to the top of the mesa. He wasn't sure it went all the way up, but he had to move quickly.

There was a chance, he knew, that Pietras was alone in the canyon, but if he went inside and Bobby was there, he might have to shoot it out with the cowhand, and if Meyer came in behind him, Slocum and Pietras would be trapped. Meyer could sit on the rim and pick them off at his leisure. Their only chance would be hanging on until nightfall, and the chances of that were slim to none.

Slocum's best chance was heading off Meyer and dealing with Pietras later. He moved along the base of the wall then stopped. He wondered whether Meyer would see the roan and, if he did, whether he would know it belonged to Duncan. Puffing out his cheek and holding his breath while he tried to decide, he chewed on his lower lip, then dashed back across the creek to the roan.

He tugged the horse into some brush at the foot of the right-hand wall, tethered it, and waded back across the creek. The horse wasn't completely hidden, but it was the best he could do in the time available. Racing to the foot of the path, he started up, using rocks and the roots of several gnarled pines to haul himself up. He had to hold the Spencer in his left hand while using his right to negotiate the handholds of the steep trail.

Looking up, he saw that he had nearly a hundred feet to climb, but the path was probably three or four times that length as it zigged and zagged back and forth across the sheer rock face. Halfway up, he stopped to catch his breath. Listening once more, he could hear only the whistle of the wind, which was much stiffer that high in the air.

He wondered what the top of the mesa would be like. He was assuming it would be relatively flat and that progress around the perimeter of the canyon would be rather easy. But there was no way to know until he made it to the top.

He could see far to the south and east, and there was still no sign of an approaching horseman. He was starting to wonder whether Meyer might not have beaten him there after all. Maybe the regulator was already inside the canyon. If he was—and was as smart as he seemed— he just might succeed in enlisting Pietras's help. The two of them could eliminate Slocum, then Meyer, his use for the cowhand at an end, could dispose of Pietras himself.

Slocum kept looking straight up over his head, knowing that any time he glanced away, he might turn back to find himself staring into the face of Cord Meyer. And if that happened, it would be the last thing he would ever see.

Prodding himself with those worries, Slocum tried to move still faster, but the higher he climbed, the more treacherous the footing became, and the more certain would be his death on the rocks below if he should fall. He felt like a man being ground between two stones, and knew it was only a matter of time before his dilemma would be over. But it was cold comfort.

He had two more legs to go. Less than twenty-five feet from the rim, he redoubled his efforts. The going was tougher than it had been, and he was hampered in his climb by the heavy Spencer. Reaching a place where the path broadened and leveled off a bit, he took a moment to slide the heavy buffalo rifle through his gunbelt behind him, where it wouldn't interfere with the climb.

As he moved onto another narrow ledge that canted steeply upward, he could feel the hard walnut stock of the Spencer pressing against his spine. The barrel kept stabbing into the back of his left leg each time he bent it, but when he moved the rifle, gravity just swung it back to its former position as soon as he moved. There was nothing he could do but endure the discomfort for the rest of the climb.

With the sun past the meridian, he was in shade, and as he looked back and down at the starkly etched shadow of the rock wall, he could see its lip clearly defined, a jagged black line against the reddish-beige soil far below him. When he was close enough to the top to reach out and curl his fingers over the rim, he stopped once more, listening intently with his head cocked to one side.

Hearing nothing, he resumed his climb and crept upward slowly, gradually collapsing into a crouch to keep his head below the rim. He wanted to get as close to the edge as possible, then explode up and over to keep his exposure to a minimum. He still had seen no trace of Cord Meyer, but decided to assume the regulator was already up top, lying in wait. And if Meyer was there, even if he fired and missed, Slocum knew that he might lose his hold and plummet onto the rocks jumbled at the foot of the mesa.

He was bent almost double now, his legs taut as coiled springs. He took a deep breath, then bolted upright and hurled himself forward, not sure what lay just out of his line of sight. He landed hard, crashing down on a small boulder the size of a canteen. The rock, despite its rounded shape, smashed into his ribs, crushed the breath out of his lungs, and he felt something stretch almost to the breaking point.

But nothing broke, and he took a shallow breath trying to recover his wind. A flame seared his ribcage and he was forced to hold his breath a moment. Once more he inhaled, and once more the fire licked at his ribs, but he forced himself to suck in more air, ignoring the pain. Three or four more breaths, he told himself, and the pain would subside. On the third, he felt a little better and on the fourth, he knew that he could breathe normally. It would hurt, but he could do it.

Raising his head, he scanned the top of the mesa. It was littered with boulders and slabs of broken stone. The terrain was almost flat and stretched off toward the north and west as far as he could see. Somewhere up ahead, he knew, it would begin to slope down again, and Meyer could have come up from that side. It would have taken longer, but it could have been done.

It was tempting to call out, to try to coax the regulator into showing himself, maybe taunting him to the point of recklessness. But Slocum resisted. There was a chance, however slim, that Meyer might be somewhere in the canyon below, not aware that Slocum had scaled the wall, or even that he had arrived. Meyer, unless he had seen Slocum, had no reason, other than his normal inclination to be cautious, to believe that Slocum would arrive at all. If the regulator were expecting anyone at all, it would be Bobby Pietras, of whom Slocum had seen no evidence.

He reached behind, tugged the Spencer from his belt and brought the heavy rifle forward where he could hold it by the grip, his finger curled around the trigger guard rather than on the trigger to avoid an accidental discharge.

Slocum got to his knees, his eyes squinting against the brilliant sun. Unconsciously, he steeled himself for the impact of a slug from Meyer's gun. But nothing happened. Using the field glasses, he swept around the rim, looking for anything: a trace of color, a shadow, something to tell him Meyer was there. But he saw nothing.

Moving to the edge of the canyon, he looked down into it. At first, he saw nothing. Then some movement caught his eye against the back wall. Using the glasses, he saw a shadow on the ground—a horse. He couldn't see the animal itself, but there was no question someone had hidden a mount among the boulders.

Sprinting along the north wall of the canyon, he reached the back corner. The roar of the falls was loud now, filling the canyon and spilling up and over the rim. He could see the remains of the campfire. Rounding the corner, he moved to a point directly above it. Kneeling and leaning over the edge, he looked down into the canyon. He saw a boot, its toe pointing up. Someone was lying on his back, almost concealed by a canted slab of rock. He moved a few feet, and could see up to the man's knee. The leg was motionless, almost too still for a man in hiding.

The posture was hardly appropriate for an ambush. Who the hell is it, Slocum wondered. And why doesn't he move?

For a moment, he thought about making the tortuous trip back down the face of the wall, but the idea of giving up his vantage point and wasting all that effort convinced him to stay put.

But what should he do? It seemed clear that Meyer was not here. Fingering the binoculars, he decided to move back to the point where he had climbed onto the mesa. He could sweep the valley floor with the glasses, covering all the approaches from Bracken. If Meyer was out there somewhere, he'd have to show himself sooner or later, and as long as there was daylight, Slocum had the advantage.

He started back toward the edge. Watching the rim, he failed to see a deep gouge in the surface. His left heel went in, and he lost his balance. Tottering uncertainly, he braced himself on the Spencer, using it like a crutch for a moment. And at the same instant, he caught a glimpse of movement almost dead ahead.

He stared, not sure he had really seen it, when someone leaped up and over.

Slocum hit the ground as Cord Meyer got to his knees, the Sharps swinging up and toward him.

"Too smart for your own good, Slocum," Meyer shouted.

Slocum rolled to his left. Something slammed into the rock beside his right shoulder at the same instant his ears registered the sound of the Sharps. It sounded like a cannon shot, and Slocum tried to bring his own rifle around. But Meyer had switched to his handgun, and snapped two quick shots that whined off the rock and away. Slocum rolled the other way, losing his grip on the Spencer. Without realizing it, he had rolled to the very edge of the canyon.

He tried to stop his momentum, but a section of the rim gave way under him, snapping off with a sharp crack. He felt himself falling, and tried to shift his weight, but it was too late.

He clawed at the rocks, his fingernails digging into the hard ground, his fingertips looking for a crevice, something to hold onto, but found nothing.

His legs dropped away and he felt his arms dragging toward the edge as his weight pulled him downward. His elbows cracked against the edge, and he straightened his arms almost involuntarily as he dropped below the rim, still clawing at the ground.

His feet hit something and he thought for a moment they had found a ledge, but it was just an outcropping that gave way under his weight. He heard the skitter of loose stone showering down onto the rocks far below, grabbed at a small bush, which was itself desperately clinging to the rocky face.

It bent, but it held, and his legs swung away beneath him. Reaching for another handhold, he found one, then dug his toes in. Chunks of rock broke off and fell away once, then again. And on the third try, he got lucky.

He heard Meyer laughing as the regulator approached the rim. Slocum grabbed for his Colt, yanked it free of his holster, and jammed it in behind the trunk of the bush. Then he shifted his grip to his right hand to ease the pressure on his bad shoulder, taking the Colt into his left. He thumbed back the hammer and pointed the Colt straight up just as Meyer leaned out over the rimrock.

Slocum saw the grin turn to surprise as Meyer's jaw fell and his eyes got very large. They were impossibly black, Slocum thought. And he pulled the trigger.

A third dark eye appeared just below the brim of Meyer's hat, and his arms started to flail as if he were trying to swim. He pitched forward, sailing so close to Slocum on the way down that the toes of Meyer's boots slammed into his back.

Unable to look, Slocum steeled himself for the sickening crunch of flesh and bone on unyielding stone. When it came, it was a damp, dull thud, like a melon shattering on the floor.

And Cord Meyer was dead.

21

Slocum clung to the sheer face of the canyon wall for several minutes, his mind numb, his breath rasping in short, shallow gasps. He felt like a landed trout, waiting for a giant hand to pick him up and dash him against the rocks, putting him out of his misery.

Only slowly could he summon the resolve to try pulling himself back to the top of the mesa. Every handhold was precious. The rough ends of broken rock pulled away from the wall, breaking in his fingers like a cookie crumbling.

Every time he let go of one hold and groped for another, he found himself hearing the dreadful thump of Cord Meyer splattering on the rocks below. There were times when it seemed as if it would take days, and there were times when he knew he wouldn't make it at all. But slowly, painstakingly, he worked his way up the ten feet of red rock to the rim.

The last step was the worst. Able to reach over the rim, his cramped fingers grasping for something secure, something solid, something that would take his weight for that one final instant when he would hang there curled over the rim like a ripe fruit balanced on the edge of a knife, he was certain that it would all tear loose, sending man and rock plunging into the canyon in one final tantalizing irony.

But it held, and he used the last of his strength to pull himself over the top and roll away from the rim, ignoring the pokes and jabs of sharp stones into his back, shoulders, chest, and hips. He rolled until he was a dozen feet away from the edge, flush up against a stone slab he couldn't get over and couldn't move.

Through hooded eyes he watched the sun slide across the sky. He was exhausted and he was thirsty and he wanted to lie there forever. But he had to get up. He had to go down into the canyon to get Meyer's body and to find out who lay under the canted slab by the back wall.

Getting to his knees, he started toward the trail leading down into the valley. As he stood there trying to force his eyes to focus, he thought he saw riders approaching. He shook his head to clear his vision, but when he looked back, they were still there.

He remembered Dan McCrae's buffalo gun, walked back to retrieve it, tucked it into his belt and started down. He told himself the descent would be easy, that after clinging like a bug to the wall of the canyon, the climb down would seem like nothing at all.

Trying not to hurry, not to get overconfident, he forced himself to work methodically. He stopped at every turn in the trail to check the approaching riders. They were still coming, maybe six or seven, he couldn't tell. But he wasn't worried. The worst was over.

And when he touched his boots to the ground at long last, he took a deep breath, looked up at the face of the mesa and smiled. The riders were within shouting distance now, but he was too beaten down, his throat too dry. He just sank down to the ground and leaned back, waving one feeble hand, the Spencer jutting up over his shoulder keeping him from collapsing totally.

He pulled it free and leaned all the way back.

He recognized Merrill Hansen and Dan McCrae at the head of the pack. They dismounted, and he saw Reilly Cohan behind them, and Ben Donaldson and Doak Henry. McCrae sprinted toward him. "You all right, John?"

Slocum nodded. Then he saw Samantha, and he smiled. "Fine," he said. "Just tired, is all."

"Meyer?" Hansen asked.

"Dead," Slocum said.

"Pietras? Where's Bobby?" Henry asked. "Did you find Bobby?"

"I think he's inside, but I'm not sure." He groaned and got to his feet.

"Just sit on down, son," Hansen said. "Tell me where to look."

Slocum was too exhausted to argue. He sank back down, then told the sheriff where he had seen the motionless figure, knowing finally as he did so that it was Bobby Pietras and that he was dead.

Samantha dismounted. She didn't run, she didn't even walk quickly. She just took her time, smiling all the way as she approached him.

Kneeling beside him, she leaned over and kissed his forehead. Then she whispered in his ear, "You're not through with me yet, cowboy."

I was standing in front of my house, yawning, when the messenger from the telegraph office rode up. It was a fine, early summer day and I knew the boy, Joshua, from a thousand other telegrams he'd delivered from Blessing, the nearest town to our ranch some seven miles away.

Only this time he didn't hand me a telegram but a handwritten note on cheap foolscap paper. I opened it. It said, in block letters:

I WILL KILL YOU ON SIGHT JUSTA WILLIAMS

Joshua was about to ride away on his mule. I stopped him. I said, "Who gave you this?" gesturing with the note.

He said, "Jus' a white gennelman's thar in town. Give me a dollar to brang it out to you."

"What did he look like?"

He kind of rolled his eyes. "I never taken no notice, Mistuh Justa. I jest done what the dollar tol' me to do."

"Was he old, was he young? Was he tall? Fat?"

"Suh, I never taken no notice. I's down at the train depot an' he come up an ast me could I git a message to you. I said, 'Shorely.' An' then he give me the dollar 'n I got on my mule an' lit out. Did I do wrong?"

"No," I said slowly. I gave his mule a slap on the rump. "You get on back to town and don't say nothing about this. You understand? Not to anybody."

"Yes, suh," he said. And then he was gone, loping away on the good saddle mule he had.

I walked slowly back into my house, looking at the message and thinking. The house was empty. My bride, Nora, and our eight-month-old son had gone to Houston with the balance of her family for a reunion. I couldn't go because I was Justa Williams and I was the boss of the Half-Moon ranch, a spread of some thirty thousand deeded acres and some two hundred thousand other acres of government grazing land. I was going on for thirty years old and I'd been running the ranch since I was about eighteen when my father, Howard, had gone down through the death of mother and a bullet through the lungs. I had two brothers, Ben, who was as wild as a March hare, and Norris, the middle brother, who'd read too many books.

For myself I was tired as hell and needed, badly, to get away from it all, even if it was just to go on a two-week drunk. We were a big organization. What with the ranch and other property and investments our outfit was worth something like two million dollars. And as near as I could figure, I'd been carrying all that load for all those years without much of a break of any kind except for a week's honeymoon with Nora. In short I was tired and I was given out and I was wishing for a relief from all the damn responsibility. If it hadn't been work, it had been a fight or trouble of some kind. Back East, in that year of 1899, the world was starting to get sort of civilized. But along the coastal bend of Texas, in Matagorda County, a man could still get messages from some nameless person threatening to kill him on sight.

I went on into the house and sat down. It was cool in there, a relief from the July heat. It was a long, low, Mexican ranch-style house with red tile on the roof, a fairly big house with thick walls that Nora had mostly designed. The house I'd grown up in, the big house, the house we called ranch headquarters, was about a half a mile away. Both of my brothers still lived there with our dad and a few cooks and maids of all work. But I was tired of work, tired of all of it, tired of listening to folks whining and complaining and expecting me to make it all right. Whatever it was.

And now this message had come. Well, it wasn't any surprise. I'd been threatened before so they weren't getting a man who'd come late in life to being a cherry. I was so damned tired that for a while I just sat there with the message in my hand without much curiosity as to who had sent it.

Lord, the place was quiet. Without Nora's presence and that of my eight-month-old heir, who was generally screaming his head off, the place seemed like it had gone vacant.

For a long time I just sat there, staring at the brief message. I had enemies aplenty but, for the life of me, I couldn't think of any who would send me such a note. Most of them would have come busting through the front door with a shotgun or a pair of revolvers. No, it had to be the work of a gun hired by someone who'd thought I'd done him dirt. And he had to be someone who figured to cause me a good deal of worry in addition to whatever else he had planned for me. It was noontime, but I didn't feel much like eating even though Nora had left Juanita, our cook and maid and maybe the fattest cook and maid in the county, to look after me. She came in and asked me in Spanish what I wanted to eat. I told her nothing and, since she looked so disappointed, I told her she could peel me an apple and fetch it to me. Then I got up and went in my office, where my whiskey was, and poured myself out a good, stiff drink. Most folks would have said it was too hot for hard liquor, but I was not of that mind. Besides, I was mighty glum. Nora hadn't been gone quite a week out of the month's visit she had planned, and already I was mooning around the house and cussing myself for ever giving her permission to go in the first place. That week had given me some idea of how she'd felt when I'd been called away on ranch business of some kind or another and been gone for a considerable time. I'd always thought her complaints had just come from an overwrought female, but I reckoned it had even been lonelier for her. At least now I had my work and was out and about the ranch, while she'd mostly been stuck in the house without a female neighbor nearer than five miles to visit and gossip with.

Of course I could have gone and stayed in the big house; returned to my old ways just as if I were still single. But I was reluctant to do that. For one thing it would have meant eating Buttercup's cooking, which was a chore any sane man would have avoided. But it was considerably more than that; I'd moved out and I had a home and I figured that was the place for me to be. Nora's presence was still there; I could feel it. I could even imagine I could smell the last lingering wisps from her perfume.

Besides that, I figured one or both of my brothers would have some crack to make about not being able to stand my own company or was I homesick for Mommy to come back. We knew each other like we knew our own guns and nothing was off limits as far as the joshing went.

But I did want to confer with them about the threatening note. That was family as well as ranch business. There was nobody, neither of my brothers, even under Dad's advice, who was capable of running the ranch, which was the cornerstone of our business. If something were to happen to me we would be in a pretty pickle. Many years before I'd started an upgrading program in our cattle by bringing in Shorthorn cattle from the Midwest, Herefords, whiteface purebreds, to breed to our all-bone, horse-killing, half-crazy-half-wild herd of Longhorns. It had worked so successfully that we now had a purebred herd of our own of Herefords, some five hundred of them, as well as a herd of some five thousand crossbreds that could be handled and worked without wearing out three horses before the noon meal. Which had been the case when I'd inherited herds of pure Longhorns when Howard had turned the ranch over to me.

But there was an art in that crossbreeding and I was the only one who really understood it. You just didn't throw a purebred Hereford bull in with a bunch of crossbred cows and let him do the deciding. No, you had to keep herd books and watch your bloodlines and breed for a certain conformation that would give you the most beef per pound of cow. As a result, our breeding program had produced cattle that we easily sold to the Northern markets for nearly twice what my stubborn neighbors were getting for their cattle.

I figured to go over to the big house and show the note to my brothers and Howard and see what they thought, but I didn't figure to go until after supper. It had always been our custom, even after my marriage, for all of us to gather in the big room that was about half office and half sitting room and sit around discussing the day's events and having a few after-supper drinks. It was also then when, if anybody had any proposals, they could present them to me for my approval. Norris ran the business end of our affairs, but he couldn't make a deal over a thousand dollars without my say-so. Of course that was generally just a formality since his was the better judgment in such matters. But there had to be just one boss and that was me. As I say, a situation I was finding more and more wearisome.

I thought to go up to the house about seven of the evening. Juanita would have fixed my supper and they would have had theirs, and we'd all be relaxed and I could show them the note and get their opinion. Personally, I thought it was somebody's idea of a prank. If you are going to kill a man it ain't real good policy to warn him in advance.

About seven I set out walking toward the big house. It was just coming dusk and there was a nice breeze blowing in from the gulf. I kept three saddle horses in the little corral behind my house, but I could walk the half mile in just about the same time as it would take me to get up a horse and get him saddled and bridled. Besides, the evening was pleasant and I felt the need to stretch my legs.

I let myself into the house through the back door, passed the door to the dining room, and then turned left into the big office. Dad was sitting in his rocking chair near to the door of the little bedroom he occupied. Norris was working at some papers on his side of the big double desk we shared. Ben was in a straight-backed chair he had tilted back against the wall. The whiskey was on the table next to Ben. When I came in the room he said, "Well, well. If it ain't the deserted bridegroom. Taken to loping your mule yet?"

I made a motion as if to kick the chair out from under him and said, "Shut up, Ben. You'd be the one to know about that."

Howard said, "Any word from Nora yet, son?"

I shook my head. "Naw. I told her to go and enjoy herself and not worry about writing me." I poured myself out a drink and then went and sat in a big easy chair that was against the back wall. Norris looked up from his work and said, "Justa, how much higher are you going to let this cattle market go before you sell off some beef?"

"About a week," I said. "Maybe a little longer."

"Isn't that sort of taking a gamble? The bottom could fall out of this market any day."

"Norris, didn't anybody ever tell you that ranching was a gamble?"

"Yes," he said, "I believe you've mentioned that three or four hundred times. But the point is I could use the cash right now. There's a new issue of U.S. treasury bonds that are paying four percent. Those cattle we should be shipping right now are about to reach the point of diminishing returns."

Ben said, "Whatever in the hell that means."

I said, "I'll think it over." I ragged Norris a good deal and got him angry at every good opportunity, but I generally listened when he was talking about money.

After that Ben and I talked about getting some fresh blood in the horse herd. The hard work was done for the year but some of our mounts were getting on and we'd been crossbreeding within the herd too long. I told Ben I thought he ought to think about getting a few good Morgan studs and breeding them in with some of our younger quarter horse mares. For staying power there was nothing like a Morgan. And if you crossed that with the quick speed of a quarter horse you had something that would stay with you all day under just about any kind of conditions.

After that we talked about this and that, until I finally dragged the note out of my pocket. I said, not wanting to make it seem too important, "Got a little love letter this noon. Wondered what ya'll thought about it." I got out of my chair and walked over and handed it to Ben. He read it and then brought all four legs of his chair to the floor with a thump and read it again. He looked over at me. "What the hell! You figure this to be the genuine article?"

I shrugged and went back to my chair. "I don't know," I said. "I wanted to get ya'll's opinion."

Ben got up and handed the note to Norris. He read it and then raised his eyebrows. "How'd you get this?"

"That messenger boy from the telegraph office, Joshua, brought it out to me. Said some man had given him a dollar to bring it out."

"Did you ask him what the man looked like?"

I said drily, "Yes, Norris, I asked him what the man looked like but he said he didn't know. Said all he saw was the dollar."

Norris said, "Well, if it's somebody's idea of a joke it's a damn poor one." He reached back and handed the letter to Howard.

Dad was a little time in reading the note since Norris had to go and fetch his spectacles out of his bedroom. When he'd got them adjusted he read it over several times and then looked at me. "Son, I don't believe this is something you can laugh off. You and this ranch have made considerable enemies through the years. The kind of enemies who don't care if they were right or wrong and the kind of enemies who carry a grudge forever."

"Then why warn me?"

Norris said, "To get more satisfaction out of it. To scare you."

I looked at Dad. He shook his head. "If they know Justa well enough to want to kill him they'll also know he don't scare. No, there's another reason. They must know Justa ain't all that easy to kill. About like trying to corner a cat in a railroad roundhouse. But if you put a man on his guard and keep him on his guard, it's got to eventually take off some of the edge. Wear him down to where he ain't really himself. The same way you buck down a bronc. Let him do all the work against himself."

I said, "So you take it serious, Howard?"

"Yes, sir," he said. "I damn well do. This ain't no prank."

"What shall I do?"

Norris said, "Maybe we ought to run over in our minds the people you've had trouble with in the past who've lived to bear a grudge."

I said, "That's a lot of folks."

Ben said, "Well, there was that little war we had with that Preston family over control of the island."

Howard said, "Yes, but that was one ranch against another."

Norris said, "Yes, but they well knew that Justa was running matters. As does everyone who knows this ranch. So any grudge directed at the ranch is going to be directed right at Justa."

I said, with just a hint of bitterness, "Was that supposed to go with the job, Howard? You didn't explain that part to me."

Ben said, "What about the man in the buggy? He sounds like a likely suspect for such a turn."

Norris said, "But he was crippled."

Ben gave him a sour look. "He's from the border, Norris. You reckon he couldn't hire some gun help?"

Howard said, "Was that the hombre that tried to drive that herd of cattle with tick fever through our range? Those Mexican cattle that hadn't been quarantined?"

Norris said, "Yes, Dad. And Justa made that little man, whatever his name was, drive up here and pay damages."

Ben said, "And he swore right then and there that *he'd* make Justa pay damages."

I said, "For my money it's got something to do with that maniac up in Bandera County that kept me locked up in a root cellar for nearly a week and then tried to have me hung for a crime I didn't even know about."

"But you killed him. And damn near every gun hand he had."

I said, "Yeah, but there's always that daughter of his. And there was a son."

Ben gave me a slight smile. "I thought ya'll was close. I mean *real* close. You and the daughter."

I said, "What we done didn't have anything to do with anything. And I think she was about as crazy as her father. And Ben if you ever mention that woman around Nora, I'm liable to send you one of those notes."

Norris said, "But that's been almost three years ago."

I shook my head. "Time ain't nothing to a woman. They got the patience of an Indian. She'd wait this long just figuring it'd take that much time to forget her."

Norris said skeptically, "That note doesn't look made by a women's hand."

I said, "It's block lettering, Norris. That doesn't tell you a damn thing. Besides, maybe she hired a gum hand who could write."

Ben said, "I never heard of one."

Howard said, waving the note, "Son, what are you going to do about this?"

I shrugged. "Well, Dad, I don't see where there's anything for me to do right now. I can't shoot a message and until somebody either gets in front of me or behind me or *somewheres,* I don't see what I can do except keep a sharp lookout."

The next day I was about two miles from ranch headquarters, riding my three-year-old bay gelding down the little wagon track that led to Blessing, when I heard the whine of a bullet passing just over my head, closely followed by the crack of a distant rifle. I never hesitated; I just fell off my horse to the side away from the sound of the rifle. I landed on all fours in the roadbed, and then crawled as quick as I could toward the sound and into the high grass. My horse had run off a little ways, surprised at my unusual dismount. He turned his head to look at me, wondering, I expected, what the hell was going on.

But I was too busy burrowing into that high grass as slow as I could so as not to cause it to ripple or sway or give away my position in any other way to worry about my horse. I took off my hat on account of its high crown, and then I eased my revolver out of its holster, cocking it as I did. I was carrying a .42/.40 Navy Colt, which is a .40-caliber cartridge chamber on a .42-caliber frame. The .42-caliber frame gave it a good weight in the hand with less barrel deviation, and the .40-caliber bullets it fired would stop anything you hit in the right place. But it still wasn't any match for a rifle at long range, even with the six-inch barrel. My enemy, whoever he was, could just sit there patiently and fire at the slightest movement, and he had to eventually get me because I couldn't lay out there all day. It was only ten of the morning, but already the sun was way up and plenty hot. I could feel a little trickle of sweat running down my nose, but I dasn't move to wipe it away for fear even that slight movement could be seen. And I couldn't chance raising my head

enough to see for that too would expose my position.
All I could do was lay there, staring down at the earth,
and wait, knowing that, at any second, my bushwhacker
could be making his way silently in my direction. He'd
have to know, given the terrain, the general location of
where I was hiding.

Of course he might have thought he'd hit me, especially
from the way I'd just fallen off my horse. I took a cautious
look to my left. My horse was still about ten yards
away, cropping at the grass along the side of the road.
Fortunately, the tied reins had fallen behind the saddle
horn and were held there. If I wanted to make a run
for it I wouldn't have to spend the time gathering up
the reins. The bad part of that was that our horses were
taught to ground-rein. When you got off, if you dropped
the reins they'd stand there just as if they were tied to
a stump. But this way my horse was free to wander off
as the spirit might move him. Leaving me afoot whilst
being stalked by a man with a rifle.

I tried to remember how close the bullet had sounded
over my head and whether or not the assassin might have
thought he'd hit me. He had to have been firing upward
because there was no other concealment except the high
grass. Then I got to thinking I hadn't seen a horse. Well,
there were enough little depressions in the prairie that he
could have hid a horse some ways back and then come
forward on foot and concealed himself in the high grass
when he say me coming.

But how could he have known I was coming? Well,
that one wasn't too hard to figure out. I usually went to
town at least two or three times a week. If the man had
been watching me at all he'd of known that. So then all
he'd of had to do was come out every morning and just
wait. Sooner or later he was bound to see me coming
along, either going or returning.

But I kept thinking about that shot. I'd had my horse
in a walk, just slouching along. And God knows, I made
a big enough target. In that high grass he could easily
have concealed himself close enough for an easy shot,

especially if he was a gun hand. The more I thought
about it the more I began to think the shooter had been
aiming to miss me, to scare me, to wear me down as
Howard had said. If the note had come from somebody
with an old grudge, they'd *want* me to know who was
about to kill me or have me killed. And a bushwhacking
rifle shot wasn't all that personal. Maybe the idea was to
just keep worrying me until I got to twitching and where
I was about a quarter of a second slow. That would be
about all the edge a good gun hand would need.

I'd been laying there for what I judged to be a good
half hour. Unfortunately I'd crawled in near an ant
mound and there was a constant stream of the little
insects passing by my hands. Sooner or later one of
them was going to sting me. By now I was soaked
in sweat and starting to get little cramps from laying
so still. I knew I couldn't stay there much longer. At
any second my horse might take it into his head to go
loping back to the barn. As it was he was steadily
eating his way further and further from my position.

I made up my mind I was going to have to do
something. I cautiously and slowly raised my head until
I could just see over the grass. There wasn't anything
to see except grass. There was no man, no movement,
not even a head of cattle that the gunman might have
secreted himself behind.

I took a deep breath and moved, jamming my hat on
my head as I did and ramming my gun into its holster. I
ran, keeping as low as I could, to my horse. He gave me
a startled look, but he didn't spook. Ben trains our horses
to expect nearly anything. If they are of a nervous nature
we don't keep them.

I reached his left side, stuck my left boot in the
stirrup, and swung my right leg just over the saddle.
Then, hanging on to his side, I grabbed his right rein
with my right hand and pulled his head around until
he was pointing up the road. I was holding on to the
saddle with my left hand. I kicked him in the ribs as
best I could, and got him into a trot and then into a

lope going up the road toward town. I tell you, it was
hell hanging on to his side. I'd been going a-horseback
since I could walk, but I wasn't no trick rider and the
position I was in made my horse run sort of sideways
so that his gait was rough and awkward.

But I hung on him like that for what I judged to be
a quarter of a mile and out of rifle shot. Only then did
I pull myself up into the saddle and settle myself into
a normal position to ride a horse. Almost immediately
I pulled up and turned in the saddle to look back. Not
a thing was stirring, just innocent grass waving slightly
in the light breeze that had sprung up.

I shook my head, puzzled. Somebody was up to something, but I was damned if I could tell what. If they were
trying to make me uneasy they were doing a good job
of it. And the fact that I was married and had a wife
and child to care for, and a hell of a lot more reason
to live than when I was a single man, was a mighty big
influence in my worry. It could be that the person behind
the threats was aware of that and was taking advantage
of it. If such was the case, it made me think more and
more that it was the work of the daughter of the maniac
in Bandera that had tried in several ways to end my life.
It was the way a woman would think because she would
know about such things. I couldn't visualize the man in
the buggy understanding that a man with loved ones will
cling harder to life for their sake than a man with nothing
else to lose except his own hide.

JAKE LOGAN

TODAY'S HOTTEST ACTION WESTERN!